W9-AZV-189

Disney
DESCENDANTS
THE MAGIC OF FRIENDSHIP

Printed in the United States of America
First Hardcover Edition, November 2020
1 3 5 7 9 10 8 6 4 2
FAC-034274-20269
Library of Congress Control Number: 2019946386
ISBN 978-1-368-05436-2

The Magic of Friendship

ADAPTED BY
TINA MCLEEF

BASED ON THE FILMS BY
JOSANN MCGIBBON & SARA PARRIOTT

Disney PRESS
LOS ANGELES NEW YORK

Throughout the ages
Stories have been told
Of herœs and villains
And treasures to behold.

Stories of anguish
Of bravery and love
Have been repeated for centuries
Like gifts from above.

But the greatest gift given
Is a friendship divine.
It's a story rarely celebrated
In the annals of our time.

When your final scene is written
And your adventure comes to an end,
Know that there's no nobler title
Than the one of "friend."

Mal & Evie Best Friends Forever After

IT ALL STARTED WITH A PARTY

I always knew who Evie, the daughter of the Evil Queen, was. My mom used to point them out in the market, or sometimes she'd walk by when the Evil Queen was taste-testing Slop Shop samples. "BITTER MUCH?" my mom would say. Then she'd laugh her evil laugh. Almost everyone knew the truth . . . The Evil Queen was bitter.

She'd NEVER gotten over the fact that she'd lost control of the Isle to my mom.

so I shouldn't have been surprised that Evie didn't invite me to her sixth birthday party. I mean, I told everyone at school how pathetic she and her mom were, and I always made a point of smacking her drink onto the floor when I walked by her lunch table.

BUT HERE'S THE TRICKY THING . . .

PART of me, deep down, was always looking for a friend.

IT'S easy to see that now.

I think once you actually swept my lunch away, too. I guess it was for the best, though. . . . My mom used to pack me mystery-meat sandwiches and brown bananas.

Anyway . . .

Those two weeks before Evie's party were pretty awful. Every day when the goblins dropped off the mail, I'd run to the door and sort through copies of Misdeeds Weekly and Cape Couture, and some hate mail for my mom. Everyone at school had started talking about Evie's sixth birthday party, and I was certain that the invitation would show up soon. But as each day came and went and no invitation arrived, I started to worry.

"You don't think . . . would she dare not invite us?" I asked my mom.

"That little weasel wouldn't dare," my mom growled.

MAL

That made me feel a little better, but then it was the night of the party, and I still hadn't gotten an invitation. I could hear the music from my balcony. I saw this huge group of people at the castle-across-the-way. Practically everyone from the Isle was there. They were laughing, dancing, and drinking spiced cider. Then they started passing out baddie bags—they all had little creatures inside.

"What? What's happening?" I asked my mom as I touched the drops of water that came out of my eyes. "What is this?"

My mom turned bloodred at the sight of me. "No daughter of mine will cry! Crying is weakness!" She yelled, wiping the tears off one by one. I was so shocked I actually wasn't sad anymore. My mom's rage had a way of outshining everything else, like a PERFECT FULL MOON.

"NO ONE will disrespect us this way!"

She glared down at the crowd.

"EVIL QUEEN!" she yelled, and the music slowly faded to silence. "You dare have a party and NOT invite the ruler of the Isle and her daughter?"

The Evil Queen glanced around and giggled. "Oh, I think we did invite you. It must've gotten lost in the mail. . . ."

"LIES!" my mom shouted.

"From here on out, the Evil Queen and her daughter will be imprisoned in their castle!"

The crowd let out a few horrified gasps, but my mom wasn't finished.

"They will remain there for the next decade," she went on. "Whatever you need, the vultures will bring it to you. This confinement begins at midnight!"

With that, my mom turned on her heel and went back inside, leaving me alone. Evie immediately burst into tears. I remember how it felt to have everyone staring at me, knowing that my mom and I were responsible.

The strangest thing was . . . as much as I'd wanted revenge, I didn't feel better. Not even a little bit.

That night and the week after were the absolute **worst**.

My mom kept going to the front door, opening it, and stepping out. Within two seconds we'd hear Maleficent's terrifying shouts echo down the street, telling us to stay inside.

Sometimes we'd see her evil henchmen lurking on the sidewalk.

I've told you this
before, Mal, but I never
understood why my mom
didn't want to invite you!
You always had the best hair
out of everyone
on the Isle, even before
you dyed it purple!

And your lashes—totally natural.
You should get some kind of
award for them.

And I know this doesn't make it any better, but I actually did have an invitation for you. I'd filled one out with your name on it, just like I did for the rest of the kids on the Isle, and added it to the stack. My mom was the one who pulled it out and said no.

(Actually, she said, "YOU DON'T MEAN MAL, DAUGHTER OF MALEFICENT?! ARE YOU OUT OF YOUR PRETTY LITTLE HEAD?!")

It's eleven years late, I know, but I found it tucked away in the back of my sketchbook. Thought you might want to see. . . .

LET'S HAVE A
WICKED GOOD TIME
IT'S EVIE'S SIXTH BIRTHDAY
JOIN US SATURDAY,
OCTOBER 11 AT
THE CASTLE-ACROSS-THE-WAY
FROM EIGHT O'CLOCK
UNTIL THE VULTURES SWARM
BE THERE OR ELSE

THE BEST AND THE WORST THINGS ABOUT BEING CASTLE-SCHOOLED

Totally NOT trying to make you feel guilty, Mal, but those ten years stuck inside mom's castle were pretty dark. Like, literally—I never saw the sun. How do you think I got so good at using bronzer?

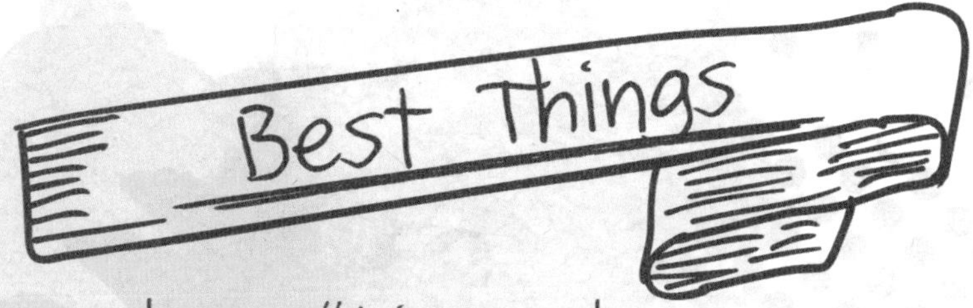

Best Things

- I was always #1 in my class.
- I could sit anywhere at lunch.
- I slept late every day, and we started school whenever I wanted.
- I got really good at entertaining myself with sketching and sewing designs, and doing my makeup and hair.

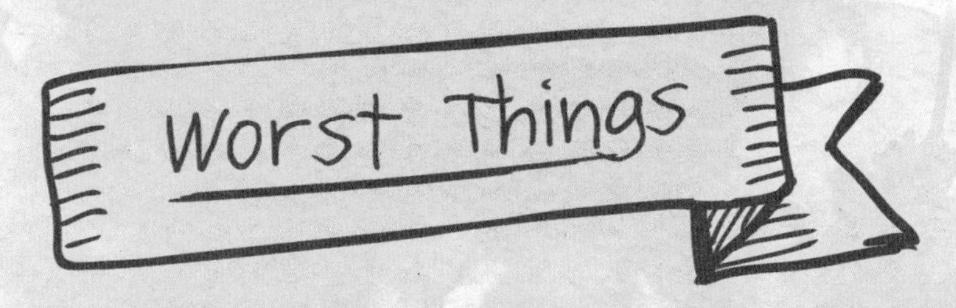

Worst Things

- I only had my mother to talk to.
- Three fourths of the curriculum was about being beautiful and finding a handsome prince.
- I didn't get to go outside.
- The vultures that brought us supplies were mean, and they never got our orders right.
- I was really, really lonely.

Then We Became Friends

Ugh, Evie.

It's really painful to think of you growing up in that dank castle, with your mom rattling on about handsome princes and how to marry rich.

It's a miracle you turned into such an amazing person—that we all did.

We didn't exactly have the best start.

And really, the worst part is that while my mom was ranting about how horrible your mother was, I was stuck in my own castle, feeling just as lonely.

I wish we could somehow go back in time and be friends then. We needed each other, even if we didn't know it yet.

Mal, do you remember when we first met for real?

It was my first day of school at Dragon Hall, after the ten-year imprisonment had finally ended. It was all so new to me. I couldn't remember being around that many people—it was so loud. Even when my mom yelled about things, it never sounded like that.

I sat at this desk with a huge cauldron, waiting for class to begin. Everyone was staring at me, and I thought it was just because I was new. But then you walked in, Mal, and everyone snickered, like I was vulture meat just for sitting at your desk.

It took me a second to realize who you were. But what I did notice, immediately, was your outfit. You always had one of the best fashion senses on the Isle. Anyone can buy a used jacket off the goblins on the wharf, but what I noticed was the asymmetrical zippers on yours. You'd ripped the hem at this odd angle, and it made you look taller. . . and gave you edge. I was impressed.

Then there was your hair.
This dark purple color that made
your green eyes pop. Most people
on the Isle couldn't pull that off,
but you did. I had to remind myself
that I should be scared.
I kept telling myself: don't
make her mad!

I remember that day.

Of course I do.

**And it's weird now, looking back,
because I don't even recognize myself.
I can't believe I'd ever do or say
those things. Like, how could I ever
see you—sweet, talented,
smart Evie—as an enemy?**

**How could I ever
be mean to my best friend?**

There was so much pressure at Dragon Hall. I know you missed a lot of it, but as soon as I became the most popular, most feared, and **meanest** kid in the entire school, I had to keep it up. Every day I had to find ways to be more devious and more underhanded.

Even before you showed up at school, kids were coming up to me asking me what I was going to do to you.

Ginny Gothel wanted me to lock you in the Athenaeum of Evil and never let you out. I had to prove to everyone I wasn't going to go easy on you just because your ten years of imprisonment were up.

If I could go back? I'd go to you that first day of school and help you find your next class, or read your schedule, or just give you a hug—I'm sure you needed it. When I think of how I felt that first day at Auradon Prep . . .

Maybe I was acting tough, but my stomach was doing **somersaults**.

I'm glad we were friends by then, and had each other to hold on to. It would've been so much harder to be at Auradon Prep without you.

PROBLEM WITH REVENGE

GROWING UP ON THE ISLE OF THE LOST,
I always Thought:

I'll feel better once I make Evie
pay for not inviting me to her sixth
birthday party.
I'll feel better once I
TRIP that goblin who sold me fake
rubies. I'll feel better once I steal
some seaweed shakes from Ursula's
Fish and Chips because
she overcharged me last time.

I'll feel better once . . .

The thing is, I never felt better. It never did anything except make me feel worse, and then make me want more revenge.

It was never enough.

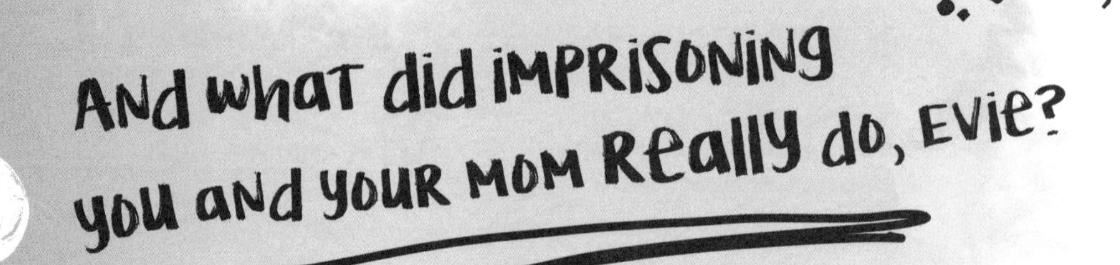

It just prevented us
from being **FRIENDS** sooner.

Because I bet if you were at
Dragon Hall all those years, we
would've sat next to each other
in Selfies 101, and you would've
helped me find all my good angles.
Or I would've made
you join the Shark Swim
Team with me, because
I always hated
swimming laps alone
with those creepy fins
appearing behind me.

I bet both of us would've been less lonely.

Definitely.

It's almost funny now that you thought LOCKING ME IN A FUR CLOSET was going to scare me. It just shows how little we knew each other then. Lock me in the Slop Shop with a bunch of goblins with toenail fungus, or tint my mirror to make it look like my reflection is dull and gray. But putting me in a fur closet? Really, Mal??

It seemed particularly devious at the time....

I knew something was up when you made a big deal of inviting me to Carlos's howler (that's what we villains call a wild party). But it was too hard to resist all those kids in one place, laughing and being normal. I didn't realize how much I'd missed being around people. I hadn't been to a party since . . . well, I guess since my own.

I still remember what I was wearing that night. I'd picked out my outfit so carefully, changing and going back to the mirror a hundred times. I braided my hair into the signature V-braid I'd been putting it in since I was ten, and it took me twice as long to do my makeup. I did this complicated eyeshadow and cat-eye liner that I'd seen on an **Evil You** makeup tutorial.

Almost as soon as I got there, you pushed me into Cruella's fur closet. Sure, it was dark, smelly, and full of spiderwebs and I didn't LIKE being in there, but it definitely wasn't as scary as you thought it would be. The fur traps were the worst, but as soon as I learned how to move around them I was fine. Besides, how could I be mad about the whole fur closet incident when that was the night I made my first friend? Carlos ran to the other end of the closet and helped me get out. That was the night I realized how hard it was for him at Hell Hall, and how cruel that Cruella was. Who could be mean to sweet Carlos? Sure, he's an Isle kid, but he doesn't have a mean bone in his body!

And that was the night
I realized you were way tougher
than I thought.
You were this blue-haired princess
with perfectly applied red lipstick and
a fan of thick lashes. Rosy cheeks shining
like two poison apples.
You were all decked out in the most
fashionable Isle outfit I'd ever seen.
But when I tried to scare you—it's like
you didn't even notice or care.
I had so much respect for that.

If we'd only been friends sooner,
we would've been unstoppable.
I'm so glad you were there the night
I went looking for my mom's scepter. . . .

OUR QUEST TO THE FORBIDDEN FORTRESS

I'd been hearing about
THE FORBIDDEN FORTRESS
since before I could walk.

"My childhood home was the most impressive castle in all of AURADON!"

My mother would say, "The throne room held treasures your young mind could only dream of!"

Blah blah blah . . .

So when my mom told me I had to retrieve her scepter—the Dragon's Eye—from the fortress, after it sparked back to life, I was intrigued.

I mean, I'd never seen where my mom grew up. But I also knew it wouldn't be easy, so I took Jay with me.

And then Carlos had this weird contraption thing . . . so I took him, too.

Then I got the idea to use the Dragon's Eye to spell Evie and send her into a deep, endless sleep.

That's why I took her along.

But everything changed
that night.
When I look back, that was
the beginning of our friendship,
of us all becoming inseparable.
Because it's hard to be drowning in sand
with someone and not have different feelings
about them afterward.
I saw Evie's head go under, and we were both
struggling to breathe, and for a second
I wasn't sure if we'd make it
out of the Cave of Wonders alive.
We stuck together, and worked together,
and for the first time in basically my whole
entire life . . . I had friends.
Real friends.

Now that we're in
Auradon and you're
the future queen,
and known for saving
citizens from so much,
it's easy to forget
where you came from.
I always saw the goodness
in you, though, Mal. If you weren't
good, deep down, you never
would've stopped me from
touching the scepter.
You always knew what was
right and what was wrong.

I THINK WE BOTH DID.

Meant to Be Friends

It wasn't long before Mal and I realized we had waaaaaaaaay more in common than we'd thought.

We both lived alone with evil queens.

Neither of us had relationships with our dads.

We were both really lonely growing up.

We both grew up incanting from our mothers' spell books, even if the magic didn't work on the Isle.

We were both way smarter and kinder than our mothers ever gave us credit for.

We both have fierce style.

We both love art.

We both needed a friend, maybe more than we even knew.

Our Hideout on the Isle

We built the hideout together. Jay and Carlos spent days hauling cool old chairs and a beat-up sofa that they found down by the wharf and in the junkyard. They added the steel roof and scavenged dozens of old speakers so we could play music. Then Evie and I added some character. I painted the huge graffiti murals and Evie sewed every single pillow and blanket, then went all reality-TV-interior-design-contestant on the space, painting lamps purple and green and covering the shades with red lace she'd bartered for at the market.

That orange sofa took me three whole days to reupholster. First I had to cut apart one of my mom's old cloaks, rip out the lining, and sew the fabric into these huge panels. Then I had to take those panels and make them fit over the existing sofa without it looking weird or too DIY. (There's good DIY and bad DIY . . . know what I mean?)

Oh! And the windows! That was this last-minute detail that just came to me in a burst of inspiration. Mal was finishing up a mural of Carlos, and she had a whole bunch of old paints out. I looked at the different colors, then at the little squares in the windows. Fabric is really hard to come by on the Isle, so I didn't want to spend another week trying to hunt down something I could use for curtains. But I didn't want the windows to look bare, either.

So I went to work. I painted different squares different bright colors—pink, green, blue, yellow. It's actually one of my favorite things about the place.

Whenever I'm back there, it always reminds me of the good times we had on the Isle. Not every day was a bad day—not when I had you, Carlos, and Jay as my best friends. That space is just this special place that we created together. I still remember how you'd yell at Jay to not put his feet up on the table, or how Carlos came up with the idea for that little "We Shall Rise" sign above the doorway.

The four of us made magic there,

even if it wasn't the kind our parents wanted us to.

to

SECRETS TO KEEP!

SECRETS, SECRETS
ARE NO FUN
SECRETS, SECRETS
HURT SOMEONE

There are some secrets that grow inside you like a fire. Before you know it, they're something you can't control, something huge, and you have to tell someone because it feels like you might explode if you don't.

I've known Hades was my dad since I was little, but I'd never said a word to anyone about it. My mother had sworn me to secrecy. She was worried what it might do to her reputation if people on the Isle knew she'd dated Hades. Sure, maybe he was once the god of the Underworld, but since being banished to the Isle and losing all his powers, he'd become more of a cave-dwelling hermit.

"Let's leave it a mystery," my mom had said. "It's better to keep it to ourselves."

I did that for years.
Whenever his name came up I'd pretend not to know him, and I'd pretend he hadn't left our family when I was a baby, abandoning both of us.
In some ways he was a stranger—I'd only ever spoken to him a handful of times.

But then this one day Evie and I were in the hideout, and she said she'd heard a rumor that Hades only **ate live slugs**. That he'd been living on slugs for years. "Ewwwww," she'd said. "Do you think that's true? **So repulsive!**"

"So what?"

I snapped back. "In Auradon they're a delicacy. They're called escargot."

There must've been something in how I said it, because Evie just stared at me for a minute or two, then asked if I was okay. "Do you know him? Are you friends with Hades?" she asked. "I didn't know, Mal. I'm so sorry.

I wasn't trying to be mean."

I felt my cheeks get hot. Then, I don't know what happened, but I just . . . I told her the truth. I told her Hades is my dad. I went into the whole story, how he'd left before I could even walk, and how I barely saw him. We hardly knew each other. When I was done, Evie just stared at me, and her huge brown eyes filled with tears, and then she threw her arms around me and gave me the biggest hug I'd ever gotten in my life. On the Isle we were supposed to hate hugging, and any kind of affection, but I just hugged her back. We stayed like that for a long time.

That's the most amazing thing about having a best friend. They know when there are no words to comfort you. They know that sometimes you just need them to be there, no matter what it is you're going through.

ROOMIES AT AURADON PREP

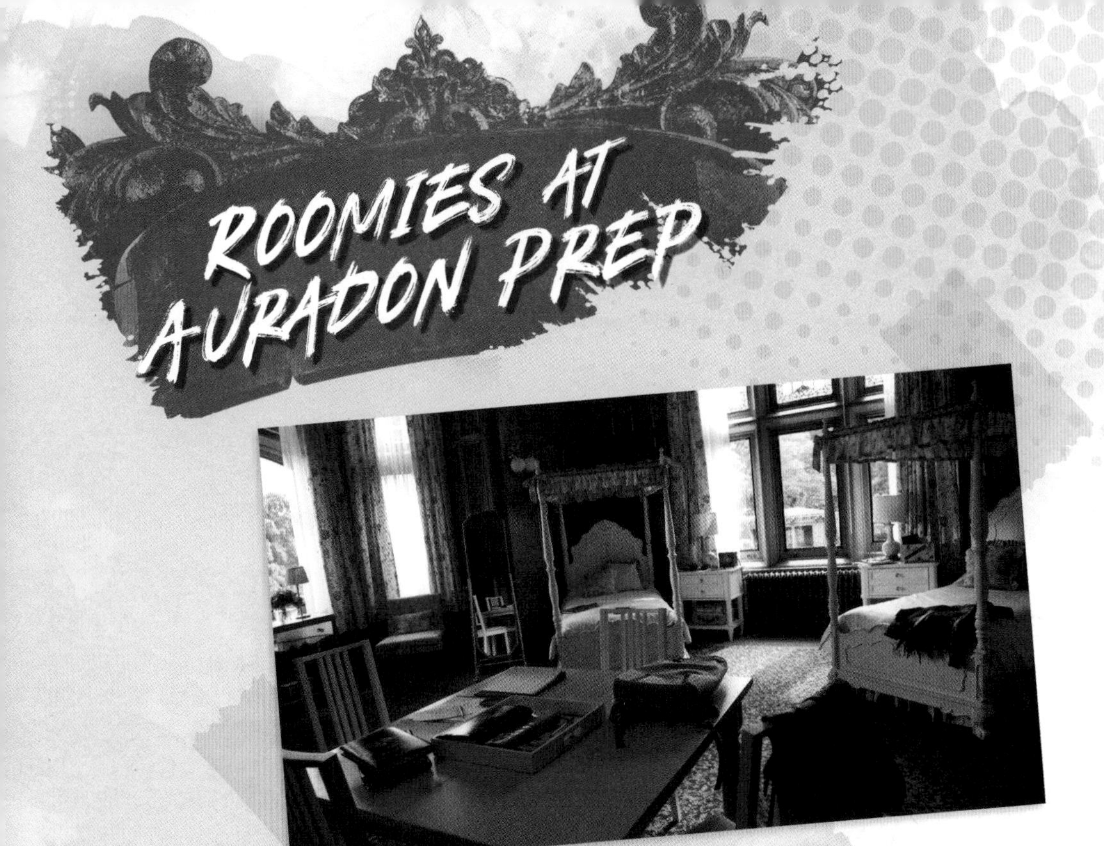

Mal, do you remember when we first walked into our dorm at Auradon Prep? I could barely speak, I was so excited. Two canopy beds, ruffled curtains and duvets, fluffy pillows that weren't stuffed with rags, a huge desk facing a window. There was so much light! There was so much green! Trees and grass and flowers like I'd never seen before!

YOU ALWAYS loved how cheery it was. IT TOOK me a while TO get used TO. . . .

It was the first time I'd ever had a room like that. Everything in the Castle-Across-the-Way screamed MISERY!!! This was totally different.

When I think about our first day at Auradon Prep, I remember you squeezing my hand in the limo, and how bright and beautiful everything was as soon as we stepped out onto the quad. But I also remember this one specific moment in the foyer, when Ben introduced us to Doug.

I can still picture his face when he first saw you. His eyes lit up and his cheeks turned pink. He started stammering like he'd never talked to a girl before. You might not have noticed it, but I think he loved you as soon as he saw you. And he hasn't stopped since.

AWWWW, that makes me so happy!

SURVIVING REMEDIAL GOODNESS

Sure, now I know that taking Remedial Goodness was completely necessary, and we shouldn't have made jokes and passed notes through the entire course, but during those first weeks at Auradon Prep, it was torture.

Fairy Godmother would ask something like, "What should you do if you see an old lady crossing the street?"

Jay would shout something like, "Grab her purse!"

Then FAIRY GODMOTHER would flash this stiff, forced smile and correct him. The answer was always something a normal Auradon kid would find obvious, like "help her with her groceries," but it would take us about five hundred guesses to get it right. I finally just started picking the answer that sounded the least fun. That seemed to work.

I was going through my desk the other day and I found all these old notes we used to pass back and forth, Evie. Can you even believe we cared about CHAD? It feels like that happened centuries ago.

Mal, don't be mad. But Chad asked me to help him with his chemistry homework again. There's something about those big blue eyes and his floppy blond hair that I can't resist. He looks at me and I turn to complete mush.

I've decided if you squint when you look at him, he's the perfect combination of Prince Charming and Hercules.

Did you hear That?

Fairy Godmother just mentioned her wand again, saying that it's one of the most powerful artifacts in Auradon. What I don't get is why she'd ever let them lock it away in the Museum of Cultural History. I mean, who cares if there's no magic allowed here?! She's such a rule follower!!
They'll have to pry my spell book from me kicking and screaming.

Fairy Godmother would never say no to Beast and Belle . . . she's so loyal to them. More faithful than Lumiere or Cogsworth—and they were spelled for decades!

A LITTLE HELP GOING EDGY GLAM

It was right before my first date with Ben, when he took me on that picnic by the Enchanted Lake. I was so nervous, and you just looked at me, Evie, and knew exactly what I needed . . .

Blush.
A little lip gloss.
A pep talk and
some **extra** confidence.

When I think back, that was the start of it. It seemed so natural how you became my personal stylist and confidante for every single event I went to in Auradon. I always felt better when you were there to say,

"You look awesome, Mal. You're going to do great."

HOW EVIE'S 4 HEARTS BEGAN

I think that's when the idea for Evie's 4 Hearts started forming in my mind. It was so fun to style you for different occasions. In Auradon there are so many more resources—places to get fabrics and supplies that I'd never been able to get before.

All of a sudden sewing and designing were so much easier, and even more fun than they had ever been before. I was really changing the style at school with every new look I created.

I found this old drawing in my new studio. It must've fallen out of one of my sketchbooks.

Do you remember this look??

You're so talented, Evie.
You've always told me the truth,
even if it was hard.
If it hadn't been for you, I might not have had
the courage to open up Auradon
once and for all. To take a stand for
all the kids on the Isle of the Lost, and all
the villains who deserve a second chance.

You've always been the voice in my head
pushing me to do better
and reminding me of who
I really am, deep down.

I guess what I'M TRYING

To say is . . .

Thank you

Right back at you, Mal.

Future Queen Mal BRINGS DOWN THE BARRIER

Auradon and the Isle of the Lost Connected

In a historic moment, Lady Mal declared peace between Auradon and the Isle of the Lost. A bridge connecting the two realms joined together, and citizens rejoiced throughout the land, dancing and celebrating well into the night.

The declaration came just hours after Hades, the god of the Underworld, used his powers to save Princess Audrey. Audrey fell into a deep sleep after stealing Maleficent's scepter, cursing all of Auradon and turning many of its citizens to stone. Lady Mal's decision has been seen by many as a celebration of the talents and skills villains on the Isle possess, and her desire to find new ways to collaborate with them. She says she's confident the villains and their families, now that they've been afforded the chance, will choose good.

Sneezy, one of the Seven Dwarfs, who was found dancing in the streets near Belle's Harbor at midnight, stopped briefly to tell us his feelings on the matter. "I promise you one thing," he said. "Auradon just got a lot more fun!"

Then he broke off into a sneezing fit, using his shirt as a tissue.

I'm so much better because of you!

Dizzy Tremaine & Celia Facilier

Forever Friends

A LITTLE SOMETHING EXTRA

I must've spent a whole month working on my **fortune-telling outfit**. My dad tried to help, but he's just a dad, you know what I'm saying? He's got style, but it's the style of a forty-year-old man.

I kept looking in the mirror, and I knew I needed something extra. Something to make the outfit **pop**. I'd found this short, colorful coat in the market, and I glued some patterned pieces of fabric onto it. I used an old red ribbon for my tie, and then I wanted to paint some details onto my pants and sleeves. "You should go ask Dizzy Tremaine if you can use some of the dyes from her grandma's hair salon," my dad said. "That shop is the most colorful place on the Isle. **Makes me wish I had hair!**"

Dizzy seemed cool. I mean, I'd passed her in school a dozen times before, and you couldn't miss Curl Up & Dye or all the wild green/red/blue/purple-haired Isle folks who strode out of there. When I walked in, she was just finishing up Mother Gothel's perm. I didn't dare say anything about using Grandma Tremaine's supplies in front of that nosy old bag.

"You think you could spare some dye, or even paint?" I finally said as Dizzy washed out the sink. I'd brought the pants with me in case she wanted to see them. I held them up to show her.

Dizzy looked over her shoulder like she was expecting her grandma to burst through the door at any moment. Then she waved me over to one of the supply closets. She squeezed some different dyes into little jars, then gave me an old paintbrush she wasn't using anymore.

Then she studied the pants, my hat, and my hair.

"Uh, thanks for the dye and all," I said. "But do you have a staring problem? Quit looking at me like that."

Dizzy smiled her sweet little Dizzy smile. "I was just thinking you need a little something extra to complete your look," she said. "Something really special. Stop by tomorrow after the store closes?" Now I thought that was really weird, because kids on the Isle are never that nice. Not only had she given me something for free, but now she was telling me she wanted to give me something else, too?

What was in it for her?

I kept wondering about this girl Dizzy. Quiet, shy Dizzy, who worked like a billion hours in her grandma's place. She thought my look needed something extra, too, and she seemed to know exactly what that was. When I went to the shop that night, she was putting the finishing touches on this cool accessory for my hat. She held it in the air, showing it off.

The girl is talented, I'll tell you that much. She planned to turn my basic hat into this cool little top hat. She added a thick velvet ribbon around the center and a bunch of seagull feathers she'd dyed purple and red. Then she'd made this unique skull piece with paint and papier-mâché. No one had ever given me a gift like that before.

I handed Dizzy my hat, and she added her accessory and gave it back to me. I didn't even say anything; I just put it right on my head. Dizzy saw how excited I was, and she got excited, too, and then we were both laughing and talking about different stuff. I knew then we'd be friends . . . or at least as good of friends as anyone can be on the Isle.

The Isle

THE BAD

AURADON PREP WILL STEAL

FOUR MORE VILLAIN KIDS

In one of her most devious moves yet, Lady Mal appeared on the Auradon News Network last night urging villain children everywhere to apply to Auradon Prep. If children submit formal applications to the boarding school in Auradon, Lady Mal and King Ben can legally remove

Tribune

NEWS

them from the Isle of the Lost without their parents' permission. "How many more villain children will be taken in the name of 'happiness' and 'opportunity'?" Clayton asks. "We need them here, to cook and clean and fluff our pillows. Who's going to shine my boots? Who's going to wash my socks?"

"There's no way to stop them," Shan-Yu says. "Mal won't be happy until every child has a warm bed to sleep in and more than enough food in their belly."

Lovin' Life

Now I was never one of those poor suckers staring out across Auradon Bay, desperate for their chance to go to Auradon Prep. I didn't even think about it much. Sure, I noticed that Dizzy always tuned into the Auradon News Network to get updates on her friend Evie, and people were pretty into the whole Mal/Ben romance (even if they pretended to be disgusted by it). But when they had the big announcement on TV about choosing more VKs to go over to Auradon Prep,

I was all:

NAH. NOT FOR ME.

It's not that I don't like fresh food and sunshine and all that. It's just . . . I really loved my life on the Isle of the Lost. It wasn't perfect, I get that. But I was the headmaster's kid, so I could get away with anything, and my family owned a huge ARCADE where I could play every single game for free. I mean, come on, how could I not love it??

Wouldn't you?

I'm not totally sure when things changed. It wasn't one exact moment. First I heard Dizzy at school talking about the applications and how she had to make sure she got hers in on time. Then those dang things were showing up everywhere. I'd see them in a huge stack in front of the arcade, or outside my dad's office. You could get them at the Slop Shop or at Hook's Inlet. And everywhere I went, kids were talking about it: Who would the next VKs be? Who would Mal choose? Which one of us had the **best** chance?

I started thinking maybe I SHOULD apply. Maybe if Dizzy was going, I would try to go, too. At least I'd know someone there. Besides, a little unfriendly competition never hurt anyone.

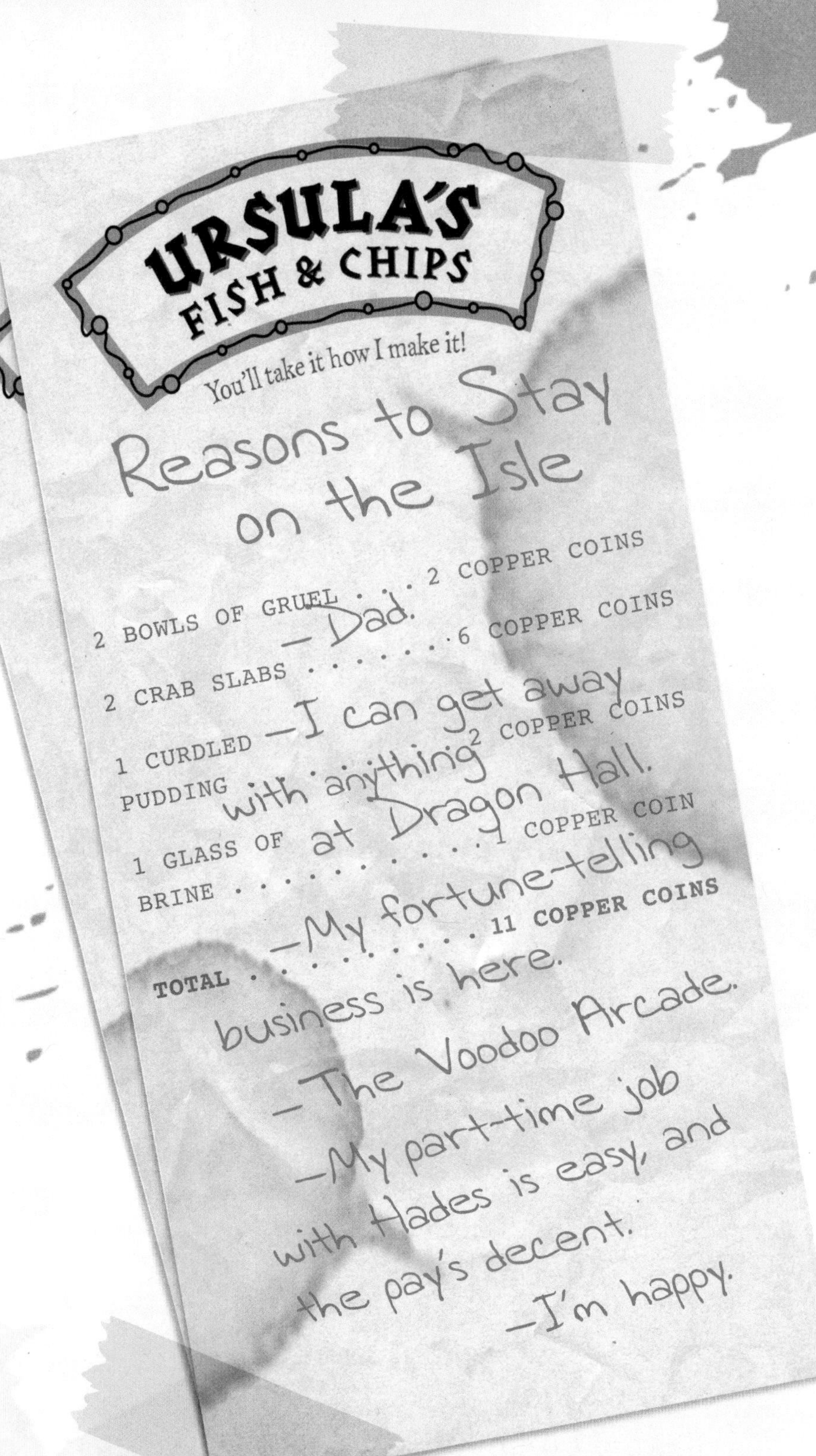
URSULA'S
FISH & CHIPS
You'll take it how I make it!
Reasons to Stay on the Isle
2 BOWLS OF GRUEL . . . . 2 COPPER COINS
—Dad.
2 CRAB SLABS . . . . 6 COPPER COINS
—I can get away with anything at Dragon Hall.
1 CURDLED PUDDING . . . 2 COPPER COINS
1 GLASS OF BRINE . . . . 1 COPPER COIN
—My fortune-telling business is here.
TOTAL . . . . 11 COPPER COINS
—The Voodoo Arcade.
—My part-time job with Hades is easy, and the pay's decent.
—I'm happy.

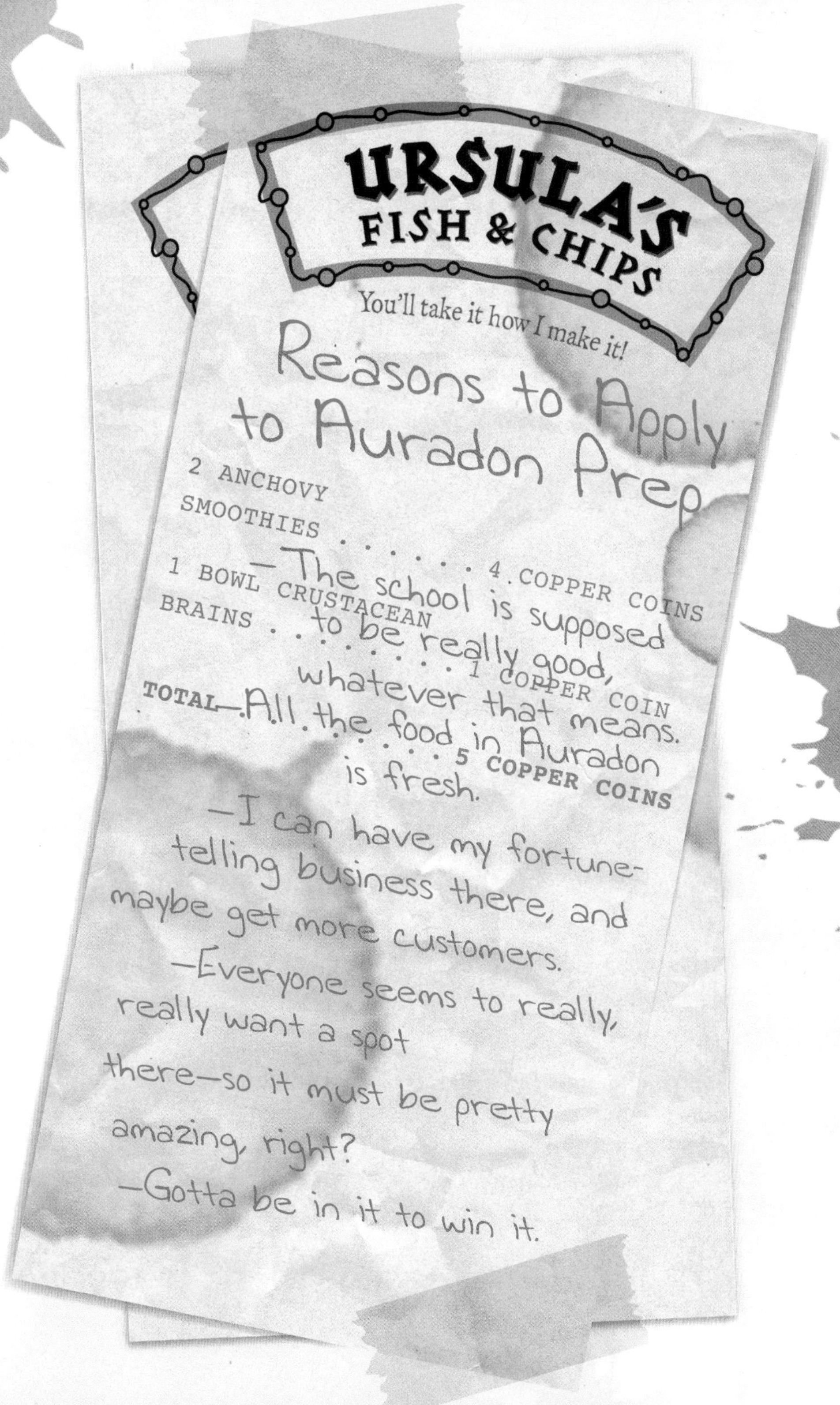
URSULA'S
FISH & CHIPS
You'll take it how I make it!
Reasons to Apply
to Auradon Prep
2 ANCHOVY
SMOOTHIES . . . . 4 COPPER COINS
1 BOWL CRUSTACEAN
BRAINS . . . . 1 COPPER COIN
TOTAL . . . . 5 COPPER COINS
—The school is supposed
to be really good,
whatever that means.
—All the food in Auradon
is fresh.
—I can have my fortune-
telling business there, and
maybe get more customers.
—Everyone seems to really,
really want a spot
there—so it must be pretty
amazing, right?
—Gotta be in it to win it.

WHEN OPPORTUNITY KNOCKS

Ever since Evie got accepted to Auradon Prep, I've dreamed about going there, doing the backstroke in the Enchanted Lake and taking a bunch of art classes, or eating in that amaaaaaaaazing cafeteria that I'd seen so many times on TV. So it was really hard for me to imagine why anyone WOULDN'T want to leave the Isle. What could be better than going to a fancy boarding school and waking up every morning to birds chirping outside your window? Who wouldn't want to eat chocolate fondue with fresh strawberries?

Celia wasn't 100 percent sure she should apply, so I was super positive about it.

"I know you'll miss your dad like whoa," I said, "but why not throw your little **top hat** in the ring?" The thing is, Celia's one of the smartest kids on the Isle—she always has been. She doesn't really care about school, but she built her fortune-telling business from nothing (maybe it's not completely legit, but that's a whole different story). Then she has all these part-time jobs, like running errands for Hades. She probably makes more than most villains do. I couldn't help wondering what she'd accomplish if she had all the same opportunities Auradon Prep kids have....

Dizzy might as well have had ACCEPTED!!! stamped on her forehead. It was so obvious she was going to Auradon, because you don't have the king's servants show up at your door with a fancy decree if they're not going to let you in. But yeah, they couldn't say she had a spot yet, because admissions were supposed to be this big process. She still had to fill out the official paperwork and go through everything.

But me? I had no guarantees. I needed to make my application shine.

School's never been my forte, if you know what I mean. I'd rather be playing pinball at my dad's arcade than hanging out in his office at Dragon Hall.

I know he's the headmaster, and I'm supposed to be as villainous as I can be, but studying was just so . . . boooooooring.

I filled out the application in the back of History of the Isle while Jace was giving his presentation on the first goblins to settle on the Isle of the Doomed. I mean, I thought my first draft was pretty good, but then Dizzy read it over and was all: "YOU CAN'T SAY THAT!!" and "THEY WON'T LIKE THIS!!" When she gave it back the whole thing was covered in her chicken scratch.

APPLICATION *for* AURADON PREP

Children of the Isle of the Lost! Mal and King Ben invite you to meet them and the other villain kids formerly of the Isle at Auradon Prep to enroll you for the upcoming scholastic year. By filling out this application form you will be eligible to become part of the second wave of villain kids that will help to reunite our divided kingdom.

Please complete this form as accurately as you can. Our goal is to welcome all of the children of the Isle of the Lost to Auradon as expeditiously as possible. At this time, however, we will only be accepting four more. Mal and King Ben ask you to be truthful, sincere and to always speak from your heart. In time, we will all be together as one nation. Your courage in volunteering for this program will bring that day closer! Best of luck!

Celia Facilier

Name

Skullz

Known aliases

CeeCee, "Stop! Thief!" The Headmaster's Daughter, That Tarot Girl

Nicknames or other

Ohhh... maybe only include the first one

October 31

Date of birth or best guess

Please place photo here

Isle of the Lost

Place of birth

What's it to you??

Why do you need to know?

Favorite color

Mind Your Own Business

Favorite activity

Don't have one

Favorite school subject

Dr. Facilier

Parents' names (or aliases)

Scheming bocor

Parents' profession(s)

They're just curious about you! original VKs their colors are so iconic, they're almost like part of their personality or something.

Think about it: Mal-purple, Evie-blue, Carlos-black and white, Jay-maroon and gold

Come on, you have to give them something! You love tarot card reading, hanging out at the arcade with your friends, playing pinball, and painting.

Just pick the one you like the best, even if you don't like it THATMUCH.

I'd add headmaster of Dragon Hall and arcade owner, too, even if your dad thinks of himself as a bocor first, everything else second.

Who is your favorite of the first wave of VKs? There is no wrong answer.

Uma, before you banished her!

You can't say that, Celia!! They're asking about the original four.

In your own words, tell us why you want to come to Auradon. There is no wrong answer.

My friend Dizzy's going, and I don't want to be stuck here without her.

They're not going to like that. It doesn't sound like a good enough reason to let you in. Just think about all the opportunities you'd have there, Celia! Not only would we have so much fun, but you could start a real business and live in the dorms, and be in nature whenever you wanted! Maybe even include some of those hand-painted tarot cards you've made?? I'll see if I can find an extra blank application. . . .

Congratulations on completing the application. Mal, Jay, Evie, and Carlos will collect it on the appointed date and announce the next of many villain kids who will join them in Auradon. If you are not picked, please don't despair. In time all of you will join us and help make our world whole again!

Signature

Please place thumbprint here

ACCEPTED

APPLICATION *for* AURADON PREP

Children of the Isle of the Lost! Mal and King Ben invite you to meet them and the other villain kids formerly of the Isle at Auradon Prep to enroll you for the upcoming scholastic year. By filling out this application form you will be eligible to become part of the second wave of villain kids that will help to reunite our divided kingdom.

Please complete this form as accurately as you can. Our goal is to welcome all of the children of the Isle of the Lost to Auradon as expeditiously as possible. At this time, however, we will only be accepting four more. Mal and King Ben ask you to be truthful, sincere and to always speak from your heart. In time, we will all be together as one nation. Your courage in volunteering for this program will bring that day closer! Best of luck!

Celia Facilier

Name

Skullz

Known aliases

CeeCee

Nicknames or other

October 31 (I'm thirteen.)

Date of birth or best guess

Isle of the Lost

Place of birth

Purple, pink, orange, green—
anything bright and colorful

Favorite color

Fortune-telling

Favorite activity

Scheme Management 101

Favorite school subject

Dr. Facilier

Parents' names (or aliases)

Headmaster of Dragon Hall, arcade owner, scheming bocor

Parents' profession(s)

Who is your favorite of the first wave of VKs? There is no wrong answer.

I've always admired Jay's thievery.

And with Dizzy's help, I actually got accepted!!!!

In your own words, tell us why you want to come to Auradon. There is no wrong answer.

Auradon sounds cool and all. I heard everyone else was applying, so I decided to apply, too. Someone told me, "You've got to be in it to win it." So this is me being in it to win it.

Now can I please take an Auradon Prep vacation????

P.S. I made these fortune-telling cards myself. I used some old watercolors I found down by the wharf and just kind of painted them or whatever. They're fine, I guess. I just thought maybe I should show you.

d Carlos will collect it on the appointed date and

radon. If you are not picked, please don't despair.

In time all of you will jo ake our world whole again!

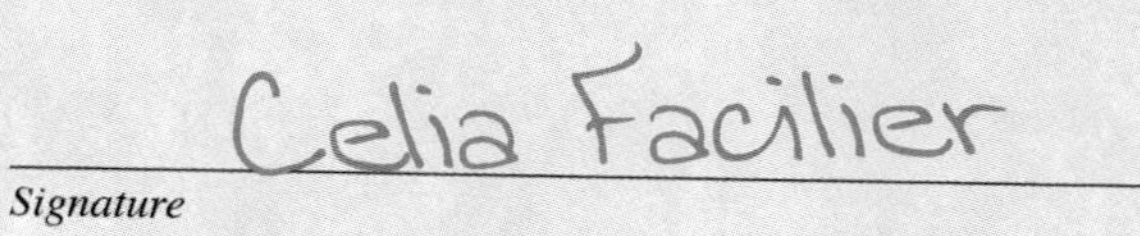

Signature

Please place
thumbprint here

THE JOURNEY

I can still picture the day the four original VKs came to the Isle. Everyone was singing and dancing, jumping all over the place, running through the streets, and waving their applications around. I felt decent about my final application, but it wasn't until Mal came down the alley that I knew things were about to get good. I had all my fortune cards fanned out in front of me. She plucked the Journey card out of the deck and then handed it to me. As soon as I saw it, I knew I'd been chosen to go to Auradon. It means adventure awaits.

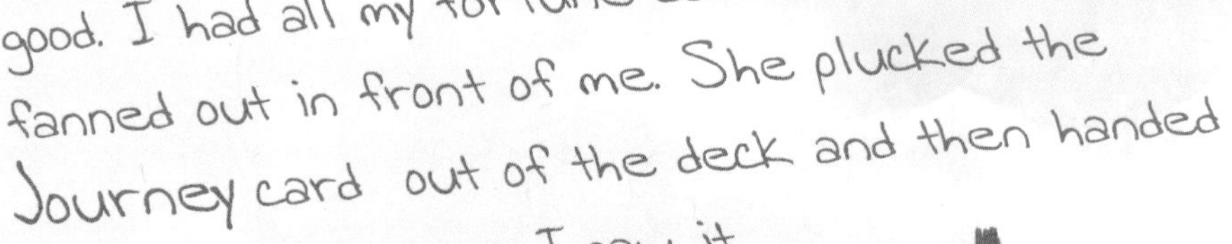

I'm not sentimental, but I kept it, just because. I still have it all these weeks later.

THE VOODOO ARCADE

I didn't really "get out much" (as my granny says) before I met Celia. I went to school all day, then I worked at my grandmother's salon until at least eight o'clock. I was responsible for keeping everything clean—sweeping and dusting and mopping and all that. After I finished my homework, I'd just listen to music and go to sleep.

"We got into Auradon Prep!! We have to do something to celebrate!!" Celia said to me. "Besides, this is the Isle of the Lost—no one has a curfew! Let's go out while we still can!"

The week after we got into Auradon Prep, I started stopping by the arcade after my shifts ended. The first time I went, Celia escorted me for the VIP (VILLAINS IN POWER) treatment.

I'd passed the place so many times before and heard all the music and laughter pouring out the front doors, but it always seemed like somewhere you'd need to know someone to get in. Like, I couldn't imagine just strolling up to the café or pinball machine myself. But when I walked in with Celia, everyone turned and noticed us. It was really cool. A bunch of Serpent Prep kids by the dart game actually smiled.

And then there was Dr. Facilier. . . .

Celia practically ran down the steps to greet him. She gave him a bunch of hip bumps and fist bumps, waved her hands in the air, and spun around him in this greeting they always do with each other.

Now I've seen it dozens of times,
but I remember how happy he was to see
his daughter. He was beaming.

I saved these from our first trip!
I ended up getting a stuffed rat
with all the tickets I won
at the ring toss.

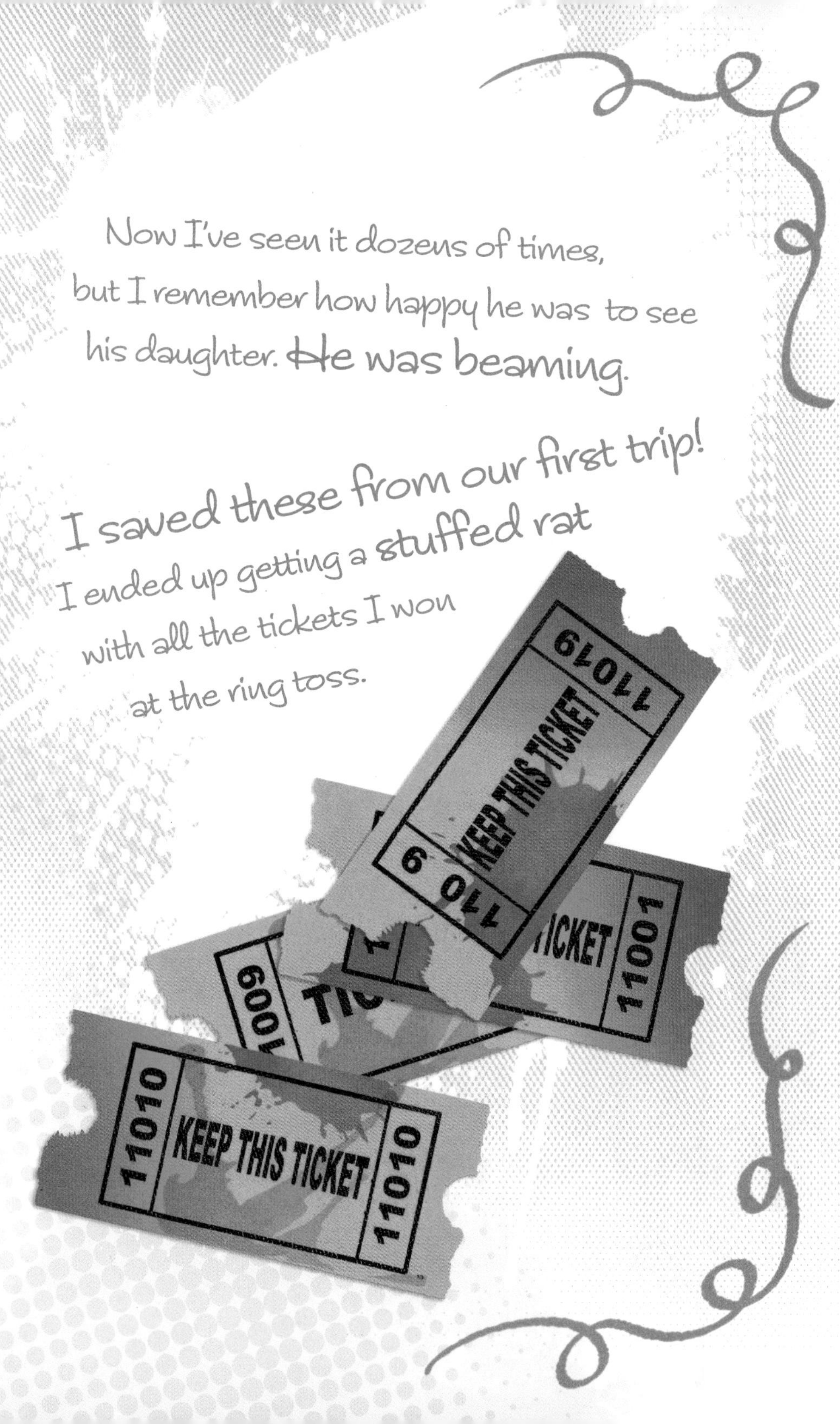

Things got 200 percent more fun once you started coming to the arcade. It's just a bummer we only had a week there. My dad usually had me test out all the old games before he got them, but when he was looking at SWARM, he loved it so much he'd just bartered without me seeing it first. When he brought it home, I played it once or twice, but I wasn't really into all the swarming bats. You had to hold these joysticks and swipe the bats away before they dive-bombed your head.

My dad played it every day those first months it was in the arcade. I'd wake up in the middle of the night and he'd be down there, still playing! Crazy!!

Anyway, he eventually beat it, and then it just sat in the corner. Some Serpent Prep boys got into it, but mostly it was just next to the popcorn machine, collecting dust.

Then you showed up, Diz. **Whoa**, girl loves her swarming bats. Out of all the games in the entire Voodoo Arcade, that was your favorite, and it became my favorite, too, because you'd talk nonstop about why it was so amazing and why I needed to give it a REAL CHANCE.

And you know what, Diz? YOU WERE RIGHT. After you get past the third level, and the bats chug the radioactive sewer sludge and get bigger, the game is really fun! For a while I ate, slept, and breathed SWARM. When I closed my eyes I'd see those little fanged faces coming at me.

Remember when we finally beat it??

It was the night before we left for Auradon, and the arcade was packed. All these kids were surrounding us, cheering as we battled

Queen Felicia Fang,

the ruler of the bats. I was certain we were going to lose, but then you pulled out the shovel we'd taken from the old barn in level sixteen. With a few quick blows, we knocked her down and made it through the gates!!

DON'T GET BIT

The crowd went nuts!

FATHER-DAUGHTER BONDING

Celia—

I never told you this, but it was kind of hard seeing you with your dad. He's always so jazzed to hang out with you, dancing and swinging you around and around. He really, really loves you. Like a LOT. ♡

There aren't many parents like that on the Isle of the Lost. My granny loves me—I know she does—but she never says it. When we talk it's always about the salon, or how much money we made that day. My mom's barely around at all. She just goes from one Isle party to the next, trying to network and find a handsome prince. She didn't even come to see me off when I left.

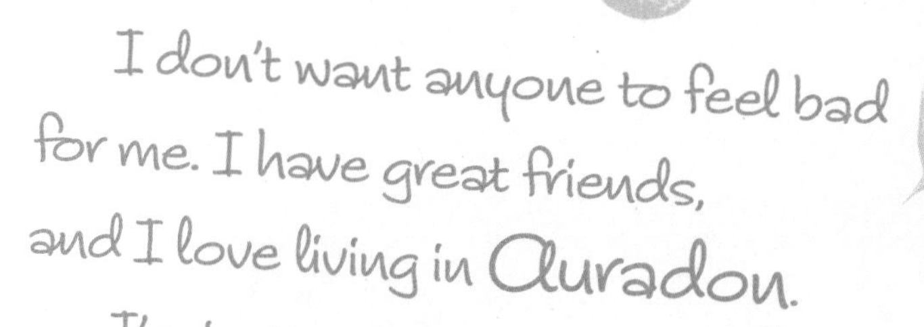
I don't want anyone to feel bad for me. I have great friends, and I love living in Auradon.
I'm just saying . . . you're really lucky, Celia.

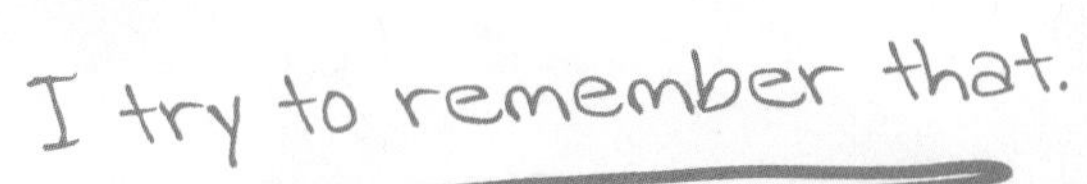
I try to remember that.

FAIRIES
AURADON

MAL & JANE

AN UNLIKELY PAIR

Pretty Perfect Princesses

When I first heard I was going to Auradon Prep I kept cringing, thinking about all the pretty perfect princesses I'd have to deal with there. Girls sipping tea with their pinkies up or waltzing through a ballroom accompanied by their charming princes. It was more than my villainous heart could take.

Jane was exactly the type of girl I was imagining. It's awful, I know, but I just saw her as part of my greater plot to steal Fairy Godmother's wand. She was Fairy Godmother's daughter, or the girl with intel on the wand. I was so consumed with what she could do for me, I never actually saw her for who she was.

Jane is one of **the kindest people at Auradon Prep**. She's **smart**, but not in a know-it-all way, and **she genuinely loves her friends** (and Carlos—they're beyond adorable). And she does **more for the school** than half the senior class. **Who else** would spend a **full six months planning** a cotillion, then smile and say **"I guess it's a water park theme"** when a giant **sea witch ruins** it?

I actually did say that. I had to look on the bright side; otherwise I would've cried over all those soggy party favors.

FALLING UNDER MAL'S SPELL

It's true–Mal and I didn't get off to a great start. When she stepped out of the limo, I was really intimidated by her. I mean, here was this purple–haired villain

(THE DAUGHTER OF MALEFICENT! EEK!)

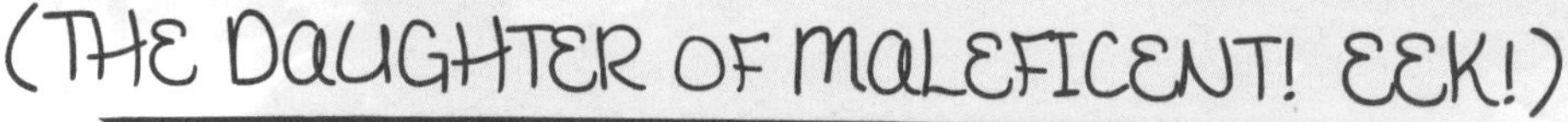

who seemed completely unimpressed by our school. I'd never seen anyone dressed like that before. She was in purple and green leather head to toe, with boots that laced up well above her ankles. She was scary . . . but also cool. I wanted her to like me, even if I didn't really know why.

That day in the bathroom (that was a really, really bad day, Mal–I know you agree) was the worst of it.

I know you were just trying to do what your mother told you to, but you really got in my head, telling me about makeovers and how you could change this or that about me. It wasn't just my hair you were criticizing . . . you tapped into all these different insecurities I had. I was really doubting myself back then.

Why did I care?

Why did it matter so much what a villain's kid thought??

I know I've apologized to you before, but

I'M SO, SO SORRY, JANE.

When I look back, it's like I don't even recognize the person who said those things to you. I was so sure that I had to be bad, that I had to get the wand, that I had to **betray Ben.**

Villainous habits die hard,
I guess....

I actually saved the card
from the flowers you sent me after
what happened at the coronation.
I even pressed one of the
daisies into my diary.
I know you meant it, Mal.

Dear Jane,
I'm so sorry for making you feel
like you weren't beautiful inside
and out. I hope one day you can
forgive me. —MAL
SHERWOOD
FLORALS

No Turning Back

Something changed that moment in the carriage, when Ben told me the Enchanted Lake had broken the love spell. It was easier to believe he was only being nice to me because the cookie had compelled him. But when he looked at me with those huge hazel eyes and told me he understood, that I'd just spelled him because I didn't believe our relationship could happen on its own . . . it was too much to take.

Ben has always been his mother's son. When everyone else saw a beast with massive paws and killer claws, Belle saw a creature who'd never known love. She was optimistic (some might say toooo optimistic, but that's another story . . .) and determined to see the good in Beast, no matter what.

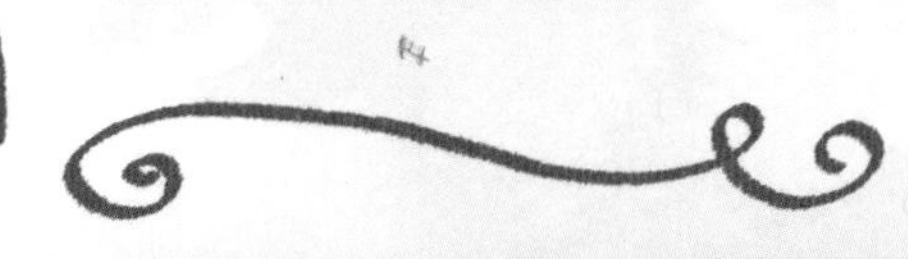

Now I understand how transformative that kind of optimism is. When Ben looked at me like that, I wanted to be better and do better. I wanted to be the girl he saw—someone who was smart, talented, and good, even if she didn't grow up that way. I wanted to be someone deserving of that kind of pure, innocent love.

Whether you realize it or not, Jane, seeing you take the wand at the coronation was one of the worst moments of my life. It was the first time I really had to face what I'd done. You were this sweet, innocent girl who had always followed the rules, and by saying all that stuff to you in the bathroom I'd made everything awful. . . . I'd hurt you. And for what?

So I could give the Fairy Godmother's wand to my mother, who only wanted it to blast open the barrier and continue her evil reign? So she could unleash her dark magic over Auradon, ruining it?

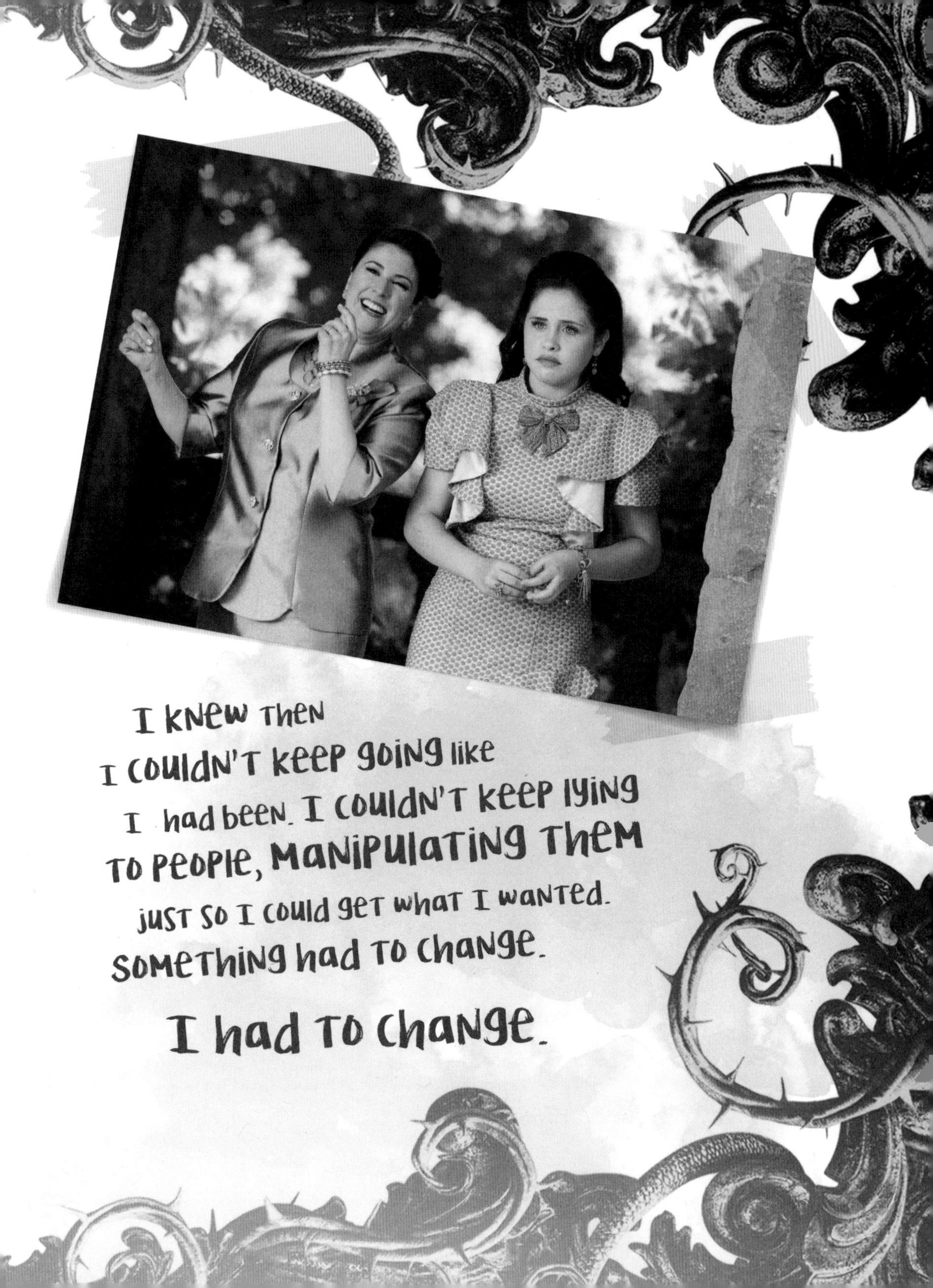

I knew then
I couldn't keep going like
I had been. I couldn't keep lying
to people, **manipulating them**
just so I could get what I wanted.
Something had to change.

I had to change.

THE COTILLION COMMITTEE

It took me a while to trust you again, Mal.
I tried to be optimistic. I didn't want to
believe that you were anything but the kind,
cool girl you were showing me you were.

I'm not trying to make you feel bad—
I'm just explaining why I was a tiny bit
nervous to work with you on planning the
Auradon Cotillion. Audrey usually does it,
but she was on her spa vacation with Flora,
Fauna, and Merryweather, and besides . . .
I don't think she would have been up
for it. Those first weeks we were
choosing the guest list and flowers and
stuff, everything went smoothly, but you
were stressed and on edge from having
so many responsibilities. I always felt like
I was bugging you whenever I asked you
a question. But then we had that day in
my mom's office, remember?

I'd just addressed the invitations with this giant quill. I had to dip the tip in this bottle of black ink, but it would drip and splatter and get super messy. When I was all done, I laid them out on the desk to show you, along with some of the different pen-topper samples. You picked up one of the invitations and complimented me on my calligraphy. Then you got the ink on your finger, and a minute later it was all over your face. "You've got a little something . . ." I tried, pointing to your mouth. You wiped your mouth and then it was worse. Then you moved your hand and got it all over your eyebrow. When you finally looked in the mirror, you actually screamed. "I look like one of Cruella's Dalmatians!" you said. Then we started laughing, and we couldn't stop. We must've laughed for a whole hour before we went back to work.

I know all the planning
eventually got to be
too stressful, but some
of it was really fun.
That was the first time
I felt like we were truly
friends and everything
was behind us.

I hadn't laughed that hard in a while. I was **practically crying**. Do you know how long it took me to get that ink off my face? I had to scrub with Madame de la Grande Bouche's special sugar scrub, and even then I still had these weird gray patches. I was hiding from the paparazzi for a week.

Seriously, though: I'm glad you forgave me, Jane. My life in **Auradon** wouldn't be the same if we weren't **friends**.

AURADON
You're invited
to the
Auradon
Royal Cotillion
Saturday, June 25
six o'clock in the evening
True Love
the royal
Auradonian yacht
RSVP by June 1
Auradon
COOL

Uma & MAL
STRONGER
TOGETHER

DREADING UMA'S RETURN

After Ben and I became a couple, my friends and I started to really find our place in Auradon. We were being appreciated for all the wild and villainous ways we were different from most people here. I should have been happy. I should have been relieved. But whenever Ben and I talked about our future, I'd stare out over the water that separated the Isle from Auradon, and my heart would sink.

I kept thinking Uma was out there, waiting. Plotting her second appearance.

I'm not usually a worrier, not like Carlos. And I definitely don't scare easily. That time Shere Khan hissed at me, then flashed his claws in the middle of the wharf? I didn't even flinch. But everything with Uma felt like unfinished business, and I knew our fight from Cotillion wasn't over—she'd made that clear. After Ben and I got engaged, the thought of her showing up as I was walking down the aisle, or busting into the castle just as Ben and I were stepping onto the dance floor for our first dance . . . it was enough to make me

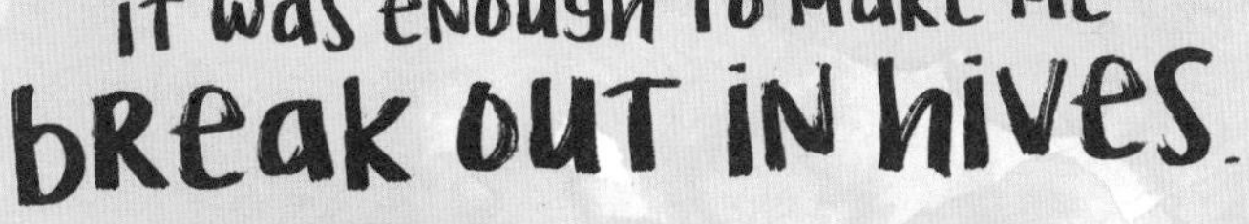

break out in hives.

What was I supposed to do, though?

I just kept going over different scenarios in my head and trying to prepare for the worst. When she reared her monstrous tentacles from the bay, I wanted to be ready. I needed to know **Auradon** would be okay. That I'd be able to **fight back**.

SURPRISE! UMA'S BACK!

It's almost funny now, isn't it? I can still picture your face when I surprised you on the Isle of the Lost, those big green eyes all huge and stunned and stuff. The best thing about being a sea monster isn't the power to control the ocean, believe it or not. It's that you can hide in plain sight. The whole time you were going on and on about your plan, I was right below the surface of the water, watching you. Listening.

I know it took you a while to really get this, Mal, but it was never about you.

All those weeks I'd spent outside the barrier, I was getting used to my **freedom**. I was enjoying it. I'd blast through the strait of Ursula and out into the open ocean, not having to worry about misjudging where the barrier was and knocking into it. I'd rip through the water, electric as an eel, my whole body awake in the cool currents. I'd swim with the biggest fish I'd ever seen in my life—these huge glittery ones that had scales like a rainbow.

I'd spend hours lying in the sun (THE SUN!!!), letting my hair dry and my skin get a smooth and rosy glow. I was eating fresh food that I didn't have to scrape the mold off and sleeping on beautiful sand beaches. I was really loving my life in a way I never had before. This is going to sound cheesy as slop shop cheddar, but I was happy.

I kept thinking: How am I going to get my pirate crew off the Isle? What about all those kids at Serpent Prep or Dragon Hall—the ones who didn't get chosen on VK Day? What about my mom?

And . . . How could Mal be so selfish, so awful, that she forgot about them?

(That might be hard to read, Mal, but it's the truth.)

It's not an excuse, but I never forgot about them, not even for one second.
I was trying to balance all these things at once.
Protecting the citizens of Auradon, but still giving Isle citizens new opportunities.
Being a good queen and still remembering where I came from.
It was so hard.

BEST THINGS ABOUT BEING OUTSIDE THE BARRIER

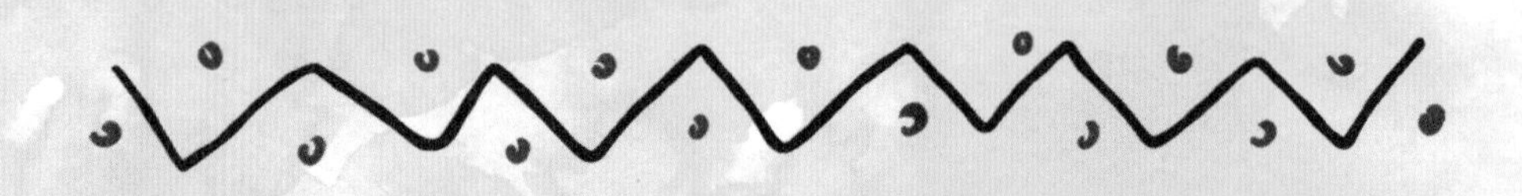

- Fish so **big** you can ride on their backs

- sunbathing

- swimming as fast and as far as I can, with nothing to stop me

• Not having to work in my mom's shop
• Furry rocks called coconuts
• NO one calling me shrimpy
• FREEDOM

The Fighting Knights

I know you can't go back in time, unless you're using your spell book (which—in Auradon—is against the rules). But part of me wishes we'd never gone to Ben's castle looking for him. Audrey lured us right into her trap, and soon we were completely surrounded, fighting dozens of robot knights who were trying to chop our heads off. We could have been hurt . . . or worse.

The thing is, though, if we hadn't gone there, I never would've seen Uma right next to me, helping fight the knights and save all of Auradon. For the first time in a long time, we were working together. We were on the same side.

There was something about that moment that changed things, just a little. As hard as it was to admit to myself, Uma had been right—we should have gone to the dorms before Ben's castle. But when things got tough, she didn't say "I TOLD YOU SO" or "YOU REALLY MESSED UP, MAL." She just jumped right in and helped us. She, Harry, and Gil are actually great sword fighters. We wouldn't have won if they hadn't been with us.

YOU CAN'T TAKE THE ISLE OUT OF THE VILLAIN!

You know what that moment in the Hall of Armor reminded me of, Mal? That day we got lost in the back alleys behind the market. we were six or seven, I think. we'd been chasing rats for fun, racing behind Jafar's Junk shop and over the roof of the Queen of Hearts' salon, and then all of a sudden we climbed down the ladder and were in some dead end we'd never seen before. I only had my wooden sword on me, this toy my mom got me for my birthday that year. You only had a toy staff.

OF COURSE I REMEMBER.

We were looking for a way out when the Queen of Hearts' soldiers appeared and accused us of trying to break into her place. They wouldn't listen to us when we tried to tell them who our parents were (no one messes with Ursula and Maleficent). Then they blocked our way out. It's like we just knew what to do. I tripped one of them, and he fell onto the other. With just a few quick swipes of your wooden sword, we had gotten rid of the other two.

Then we sprinted off down the alley.

It wasn't until we got back to the wharf that we started laughing.

You Auradon Prep kids really don't know how good you have it. As soon as I walked into Audrey's room, the smell hit me like a brick to the face.

Perfume. Roses. Hair spray. Her bed was like one huge pillow. The sheets had these frilly things on the ends just for decoration. Every piece of furniture in that place was clean and polished and . . . not broken. Like, the chairs and desk had all four legs on them.

It was hard to feel bad for Audrey, prim and prissy Audrey, who spent her whole life in Auradon. But then I cracked the spine on her diary. Whoa, that is some messed-up stuff. Mal, you totally ruined her life! I thought you'd caused problems for me, but I've got nothing on Audrey!

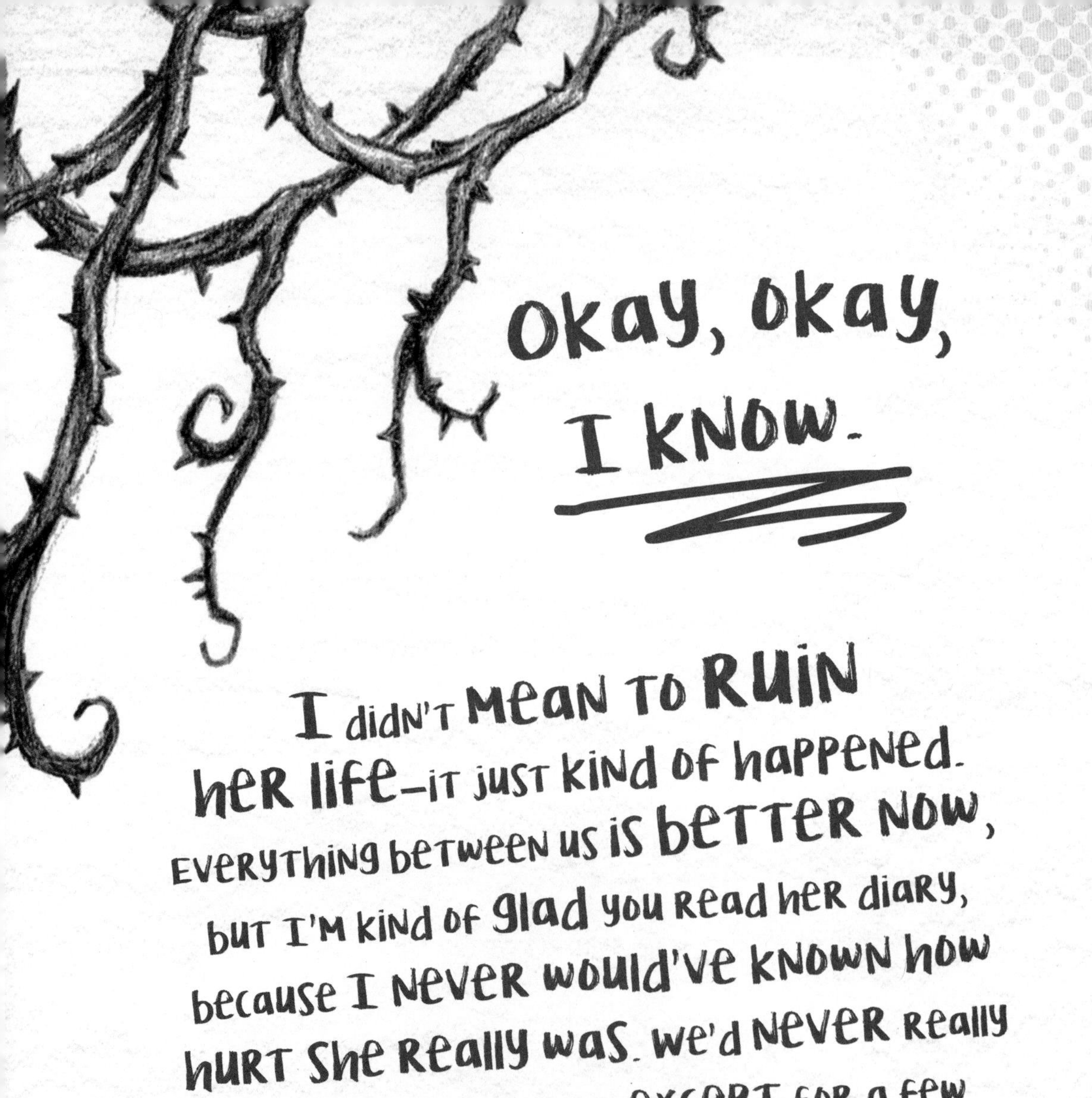
Okay, okay,
I know.
I didn't mean to ruin her life—it just kind of happened. Everything between us is better now, but I'm kind of glad you read her diary, because I never would've known how hurt she really was. We'd never really talked to each other except for a few snarky comments here and there.

You were the only one who
told me what was really going on
behind her perfect smile.

WAY BACK WHEN

It wasn't until we were sitting in
Evie's castle, scarfing down the last of
Jane's birthday cake, that I started thinking
about all those years on the Isle of the Lost
when we hated each other. You were just
someone I sneered at on the wharf, or the
leader of the pirate crew Evie and I had to
avoid. At some point I stopped thinking about
you as Uma, the friend from when I was a kid.

Summers were the best. That was our time.
As soon as Dragon Hall and Serpent Prep
let out, you and I ruled the Isle streets.
I remember pranking Hook by making
ticktock noises. It totally freaked him out.
We spray-painted half the walls in the market.
That was before either one of us was a
decent artist. I remember my seashells
looked like **giant** purple blobs.

HOW MANY AFTERNOONS did we SPEND hanging OUT AT YOUR MOM'S fish and ChiPS ShOP, SlURPING down CRab-eye SOUP?

That was WAY BACK when my mom was working behind the counter, and she'd yell at us to be meaner.

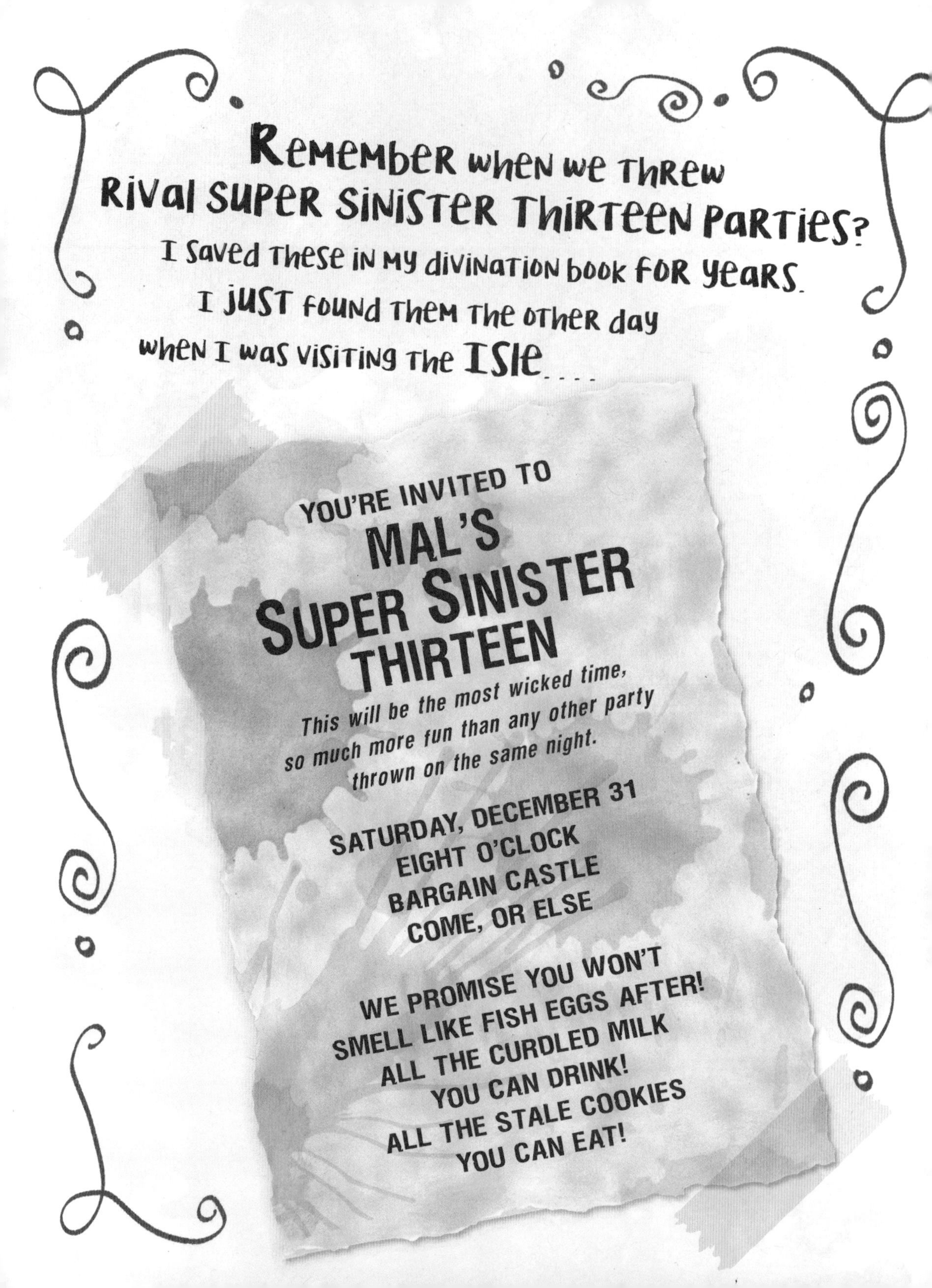
Remember when we threw
rival Super Sinister Thirteen parties?
I saved these in my divination book for years.
I just found them the other day
when I was visiting the Isle....
YOU'RE INVITED TO
MAL'S
SUPER SINISTER
THIRTEEN
This will be the most wicked time,
so much more fun than any other party
thrown on the same night.
SATURDAY, DECEMBER 31
EIGHT O'CLOCK
BARGAIN CASTLE
COME, OR ELSE
WE PROMISE YOU WON'T
SMELL LIKE FISH EGGS AFTER!
ALL THE CURDLED MILK
YOU CAN DRINK!
ALL THE STALE COOKIES
YOU CAN EAT!

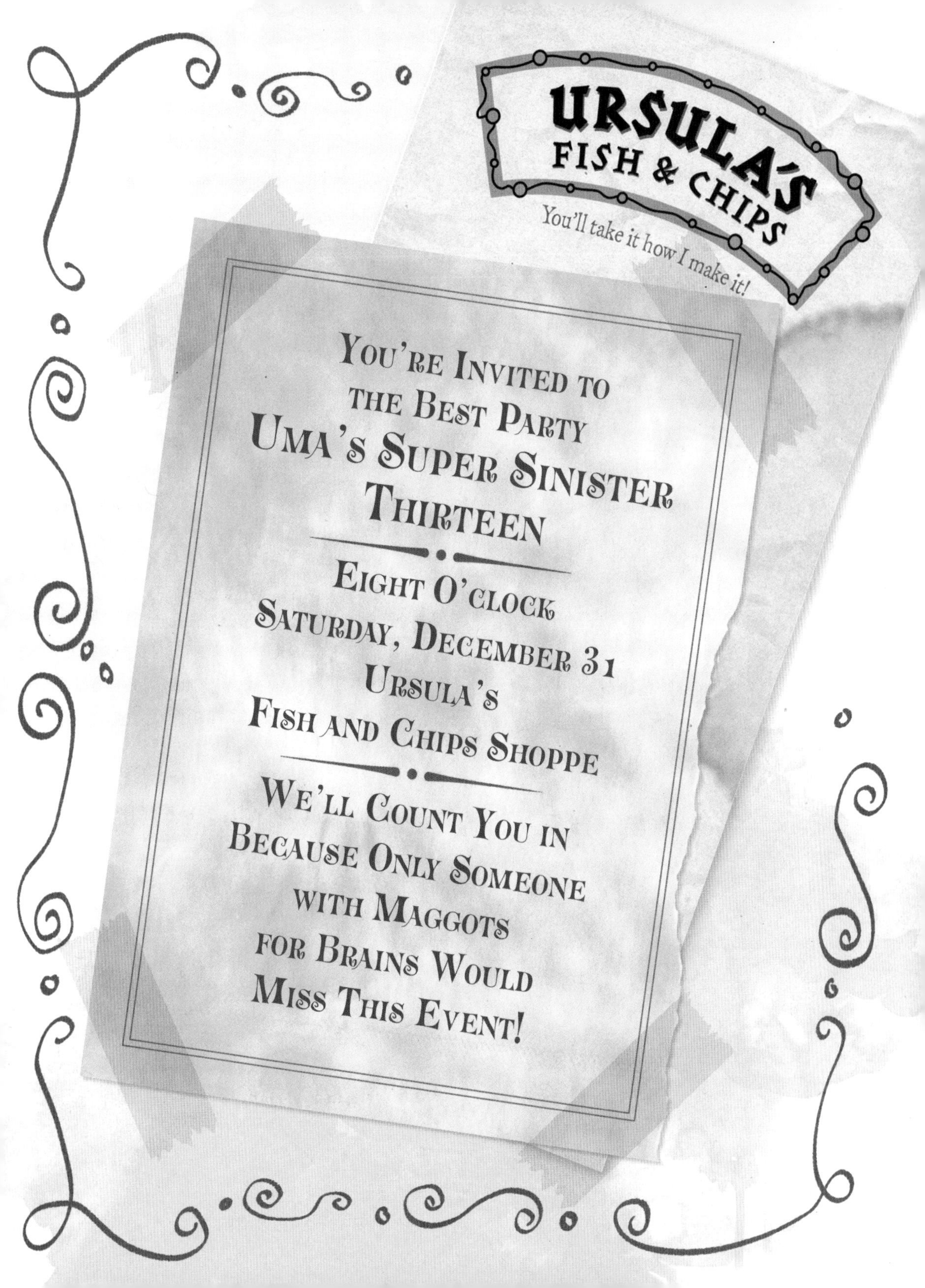
URSULA'S
FISH & CHIPS
You'll take it how I make it!
You're Invited to
the Best Party
Uma's Super Sinister
Thirteen
Eight O'clock
Saturday, December 31
Ursula's
Fish and Chips Shoppe
We'll Count You in
Because Only Someone
with Maggots
for Brains Would
Miss This Event!

• LET THEM EAT CAKE •

It might've seemed like a small thing to you, Mal, but when you thanked me in Evie's castle . . . that was **huge.** We'd spent so many years trying to **prove** which one of us was the **fiercest Isle girl,** and then like that things changed. I knew you actually meant it because you didn't smirk after you said it. You were being real.

"I kinda missed the boat a little when I called you **shrimpy** and wouldn't let you in the gang," you said.

I'm not a mushy person AT ALL, but that got me a little bit. How many years had you rallied Isle kids to call me shrimpy and tell me I **stank like seafood**? How long had it been since there'd even been a smile between us?

It gets old, always having to watch your back.

OLD FRIENDS REUNITE

OUR POWER is so much greater when we're together. You saw what happened in the tower.

One minute we're sitting there, just laughing and talking about all those years we wasted being rivals. Then whack whack whack! Wooden boards flew up and closed off every window and door, locking us inside. Celia ran down the stairs, went to the door, and then yelled, "We're trapped!"

Evie's castle was under attack.

I could feel Audrey's dark magic swirling around us. I would've done anything to make it stop. I channeled all the power I had and shouted back, "You've caused my friends pain and fear. We've had enough—now disappear." I kept chanting it, drawing up all the energy I had, but nothing worked. The castle was dark, and I could still feel Audrey's magic holding us in place. She'd made a prison for us.

It wasn't until I felt your hand grab mine that a surge of magic shot through me. As we chanted together, I felt our magic growing, our powers combining and getting stronger, and then I knew it was overcoming the spell from Audrey's scepter. You held on to your shell necklace, and it glowed in the darkness. One by one, the wooden planks flew off the windows. Suddenly light flooded in. I knew that together we'd be okay.

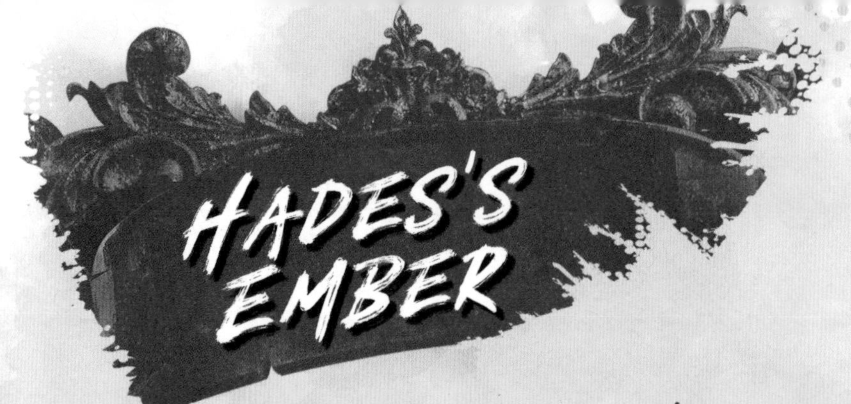

HADES'S EMBER

When I took the ember, I wasn't doing it to be all mean and villainous. Truly. I just wanted to have something over you, Mal, because I didn't think there was any way you were going to keep me and my crew around otherwise. I wanted to go to Auradon, I wanted to help save the Kingdom and free everyone on the Isle of the Lost, and I wanted you to know you couldn't push me around while I was doing it.

But after a while, holding on to it seemed kind of . . . not so great. I had it tucked away in my shell necklace, but it was never going to be as useful for me as it was for you. It wasn't my dad's special artifact, and I barely knew how it worked. Besides, it smelled like mold and dust and stuff.

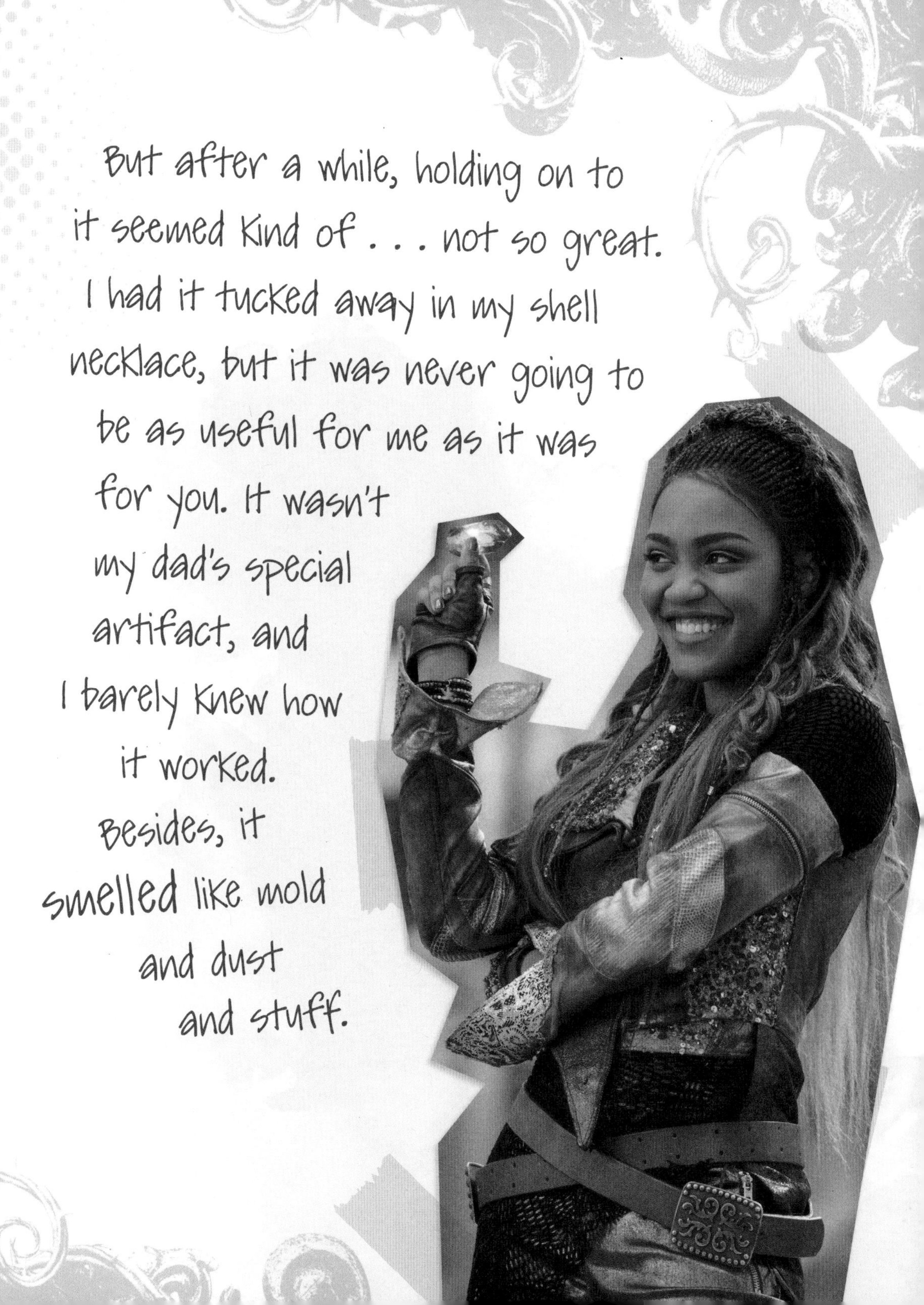

I know you don't want to seem soft, and you're not. But giving me back the ember was the only real shot we had at defeating Audrey. My powers surged and grew.

If you hadn't done that, we might not have won. The kingdom might still be asleep . . . turned to stone . . . consumed by evil. . . .

Everything would've been different

if you hadn't made that choice.

MY BETTER HALF

I used to hear people use that phrase, "my better half." It was so icky I thought I'd lose my lunch.

"Blah blah blah love love blah blah my boyfriend blah blah he's my better half."

First of all: No one should ever complete you. You should be able to stand on your own.

Second: Even if I were half of a whole, I like to think I'd be a pretty incredible half. Maybe not the better half, but definitely not the worse one.

It's funny, though . . . now that I'm with Ben, I kind of understand. Just a little bit. Because all those times I glared at the sea daring Uma to come back, or said she was this or that (insert horrible word here), Ben was always optimistic.

He always thought she would do well in Auradon. He thought that the pirates, like all the Isle kids, deserved another chance.

I guess what I'm trying to say is that he always saw the good in you, Uma. He's always seen the good in all of us. That's one of the reasons it's so easy to love Ben. He never lets anything shake his optimism. I really admire that (and maybe I do think he's better than I am at being 100 percent positive, even if I'd never, ever admit to having a "better half").

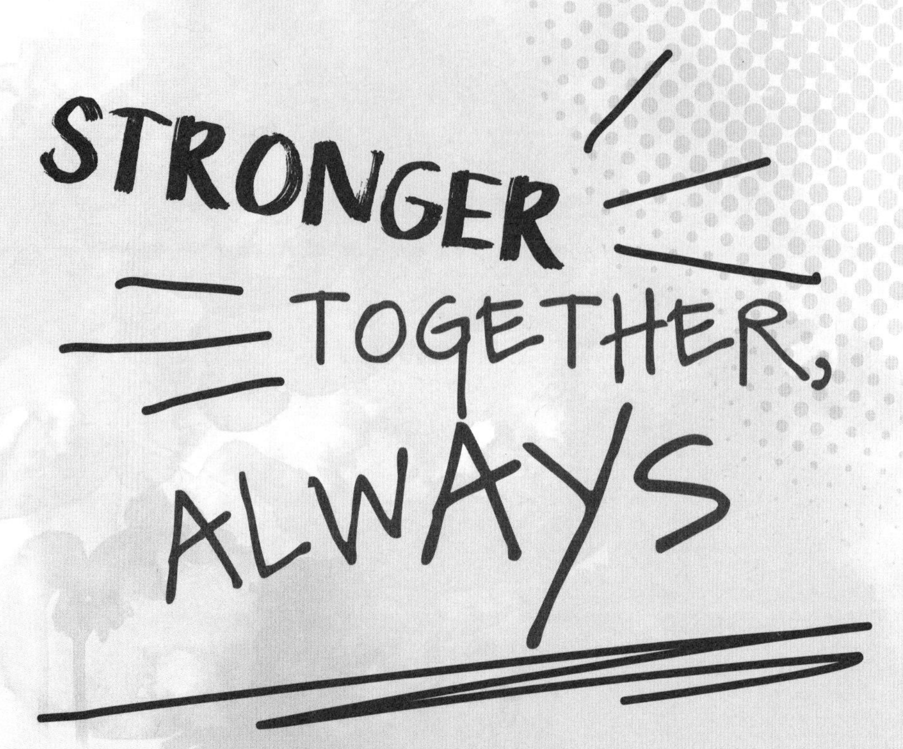

Mal, when I found out you were closing the barrier for good, I was flooded with emotion, and that doesn't happen often.

I was sad. I felt betrayed.

The worst part was, I wasn't even angry at you—I was angry at myself for being so trusting after all I'd seen. With all I knew.

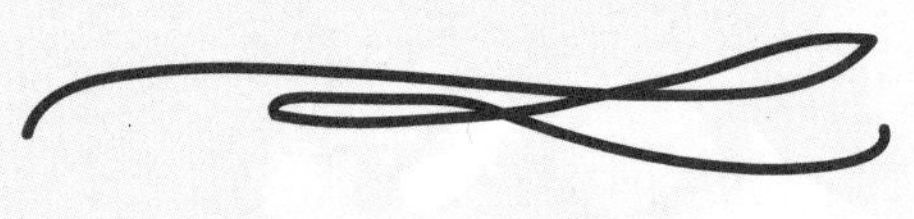

I kept going over every tiny moment with Harry, stewing about how we'd foolishly helped you all defeat Audrey only to be sent back to that dank prison. I let my guard down, and you **used us—manipulated me**—when you knew all along we were **doomed**. How was I supposed to stay inside the barrier now that I'd had my taste of **freedom**? What was I going to say to all the Isle kids trapped there—that it wasn't **waaaaay better** in Auradon? That the air wasn't cleaner, the food wasn't tastier, and the beds weren't as soft as a fresh-baked muffin?

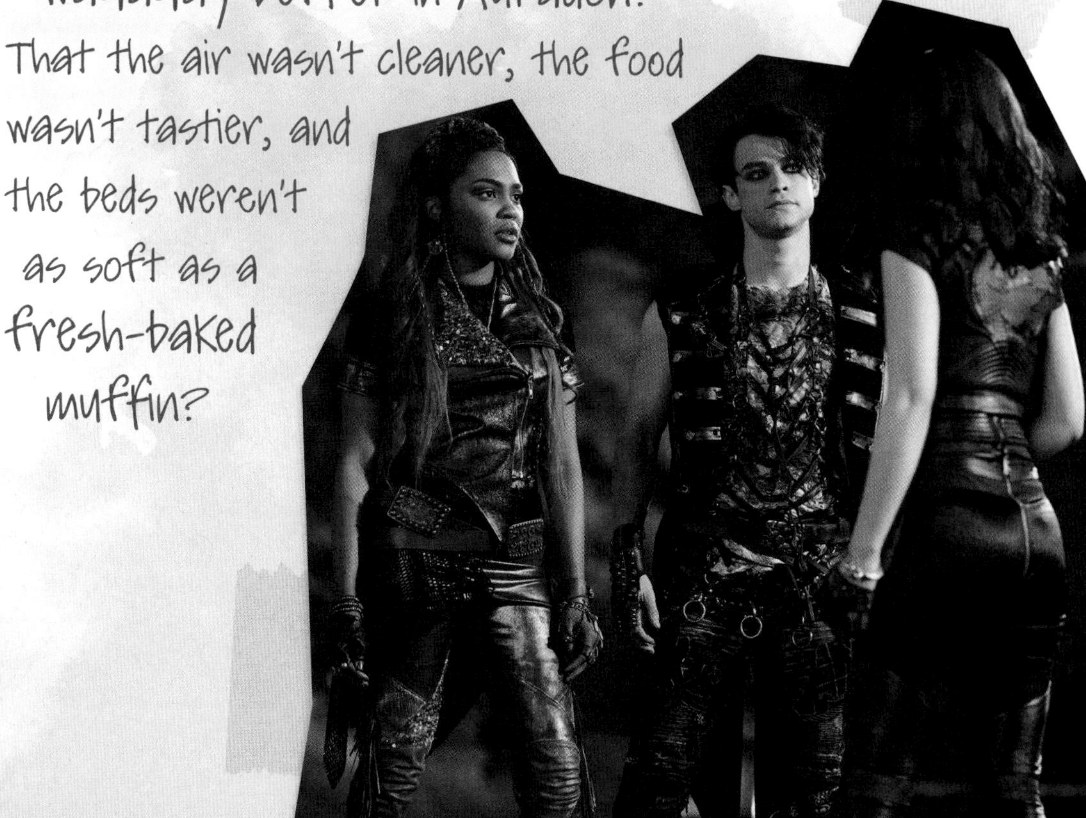

Whatever I was feeling about it (did I mention I was feeling things?), all that changed when I looked up and saw you in dragon form. Audrey blasted you with the scepter.

You curled in on yourself and twisted and turned. I could tell you were in a lot of pain. Every time she'd hit you, you'd look down at Hades's ember and try to reignite it. But no matter how much fire you breathed on it, it was dark. It couldn't save you.

I didn't think it could get much worse than that—watching you be defeated by Audrey. But then I heard Celia's scream. "Save me! Help me!" I never cry, but I got that knot thingy in my throat, like I might be on the verge.

Celia's always been tough and fearless, and I love that about her. She tossed the ember into the fountain and didn't look back. I knew I deserved to be punished. I knew how furious you all were that I'd hidden the truth from you for so long. But when I saw the flame go out, my stomach dropped. I'd never be able to defeat Audrey alone. I didn't stand a chance.

Still . . . I couldn't just stand there listening to Celia scream and not try to help. It's my responsibility to protect Auradon, and I'd failed to stop Audrey. I'd failed everyone. I wasn't going to let her hurt anyone else, especially when it was me she wanted.

Every time she blasted me with the scepter, pain ripped through my sides. I'd swoop down, trying to hit her back, but it was like I was weighed down by bricks. My movements were so slow. My head throbbed. When I looked at the ember and tried to breathe it back to life, I couldn't. I was helpless.

That's when I heard your voice, Uma.

"I'm right here, Mal.
I'm right here."

You knew I wouldn't be able to ignite the ember without you. You could've left me there, but you didn't.

"Stronger together, Mal,"

you repeated, staring up at me.

"Regain your might
and ignite.
Regain your might
and ignite."

I looked down at you, holding your shell necklace as it glowed. Uma, my friend when we were kids. The one I'd chase through the Isle alleys, or eat day-old cheese sandwiches with on the roof of the Slop Shop. The same Uma who was my enemy for so many years. The one I'd lied to and hurt, even if I hadn't meant to.

After all that, you came back for me. You knew I needed you, and you came back.

I remember so much about that night.
I remember how our powers joined together and the ember sparked to life.
I remember defeating Audrey and Celia returning to us safe.
But the part that will always be the best memory, my most treasured one, was seeing you on the lawn, staring up at me.

I'd missed my old friend.
I'm glad we're back together again.

Evie's Icebreakers

So maybe it was a little cheesy (like Slop Shop cheddar ☺), but you have to give Evie **points** for **optimism**. She's always been a seaweed-shake-half-full kind of girl.

The thing is . . . every time she'd tell us to say something we liked about each other, or that we should work on together, I always thought of something—even if I didn't say it out loud. It just got easier and easier to remember why we were friends when we were kids, and I find new reasons to like you every day.

Maybe she was right after all. . . .

Things I Like About Uma

—Her style is next level.

—She's opinionated.

—She's a boss.

—She's a hard worker.

—She's a loyal friend.

—She's always thinking about everyone on the Isle.

—She can swing a sword like nobody else.

—Her powers are fierce.

—She's smart.

—She's forgiving.

AWWWWW, I'm getting a little choked up!
(Kidding—I haven't cried since I was two months old.)
I get it, though, I do. Evie is way more upbeat than anyone I've ever been friends with. It's more contagious than a stomach flu.

Besides, now that the barrier has come down, I like being a little more . . . optimistic? Is that the word? When you let yourself think good thoughts or have goals? When you can expect a lot from people, instead of coming up with reasons not to like them?

THINGS I LIKE ABOUT MAL

—HER style is next level.

—She tried to bring more VKs to Auradon.

—She doesn't let people push her around.

—She can hold a grudge for decades.

—She's willing to fight for what she believes in.

—Even if she makes a mistake, she tries to make it better.

—She's a good leader.

—Her dragon form is LEGIT terrifying, and I mean that as a compliment.

—She loves her friends.

LADY TREMAINE'S
CURL UP & DYE
CLOSED UNTIL
MIDNIGHT
EVIE
PROOF THAT DREAMS DO COME TRUE!
EVIE took the Isle Style to AURADON and slayed!

Evie & Dizzy
Unofficial
Sisters

Dizzy's always been like a little sister to me. I missed her so much when I came to Auradon Prep, but it wasn't until I returned to the Isle that I realized I had to do something about it. Everything in Auradon is so beautiful—the trees; the flowers; the perfect, pristine dorms. It's easy to forget that things weren't always like that. Out there, across Auradon Bay, hundreds of kids are still dreaming. They're still waiting for their big chance.

Dizzy saved my sketchbook for me, and she even pasted in some newspaper clippings of what I'd accomplished.

Then she gave me these headpieces she'd made with bits of fabric and wire scavenged from the market. "It would make me so happy knowing you're wearing something of mine in Auradon . . ." she said. "Almost like me being there myself."

My whole heart ached when she said that. Going to Auradon had been something we always talked about doing together. We'd gone on and on about the Olympic-sized swimming pools, and the four-poster beds, and what we thought ice cream tasted like. There was this rumor that everyone in Auradon had washing machines and irons that kept their clothes looking like new. We couldn't wait to see if that was true.

But I was the only one who got the chance to leave. While I was designing my fashion line and saving up for a starter castle, Dizzy was still stuck. She still had to work in that shop every day after school and deal with Harry, who raided her cash register whenever he needed lunch money.

I knew I had to get her off the Isle of the Lost, no matter what. She's so talented, and so sweet, and just the most enthusiastic and optimistic person you could ever be friends with. I wanted her to have all the chances I'd had in Auradon. I just needed everyone to see she deserved them. . . .

THE PLAN

All of Dizzy's pieces were so beautiful it was easy to incorporate them in different Cotillion looks. Our styles are similar enough that pulling it together was effortless, even if it was a bit last-minute. I made everything happen just hours before the dance.

Here's the thing about Auradon: as soon as Mal started dating Ben, Isle Style became cool. Everyone at school wanted to rip the hem of their skirt or smear paint across the front of their jacket. I once walked into the girls' bathroom and found three different freshmen cutting holes in their T-shirts like the ones I'd cut into mine. That's all to say . . . I knew I just had to get the headpieces into the right hands. As soon as girls in Auradon saw Mal or Lonnie wearing them, they'd all want one for themselves. It wouldn't be long before every boutique in Camelot Heights had Dizzy's headpieces in the front window.

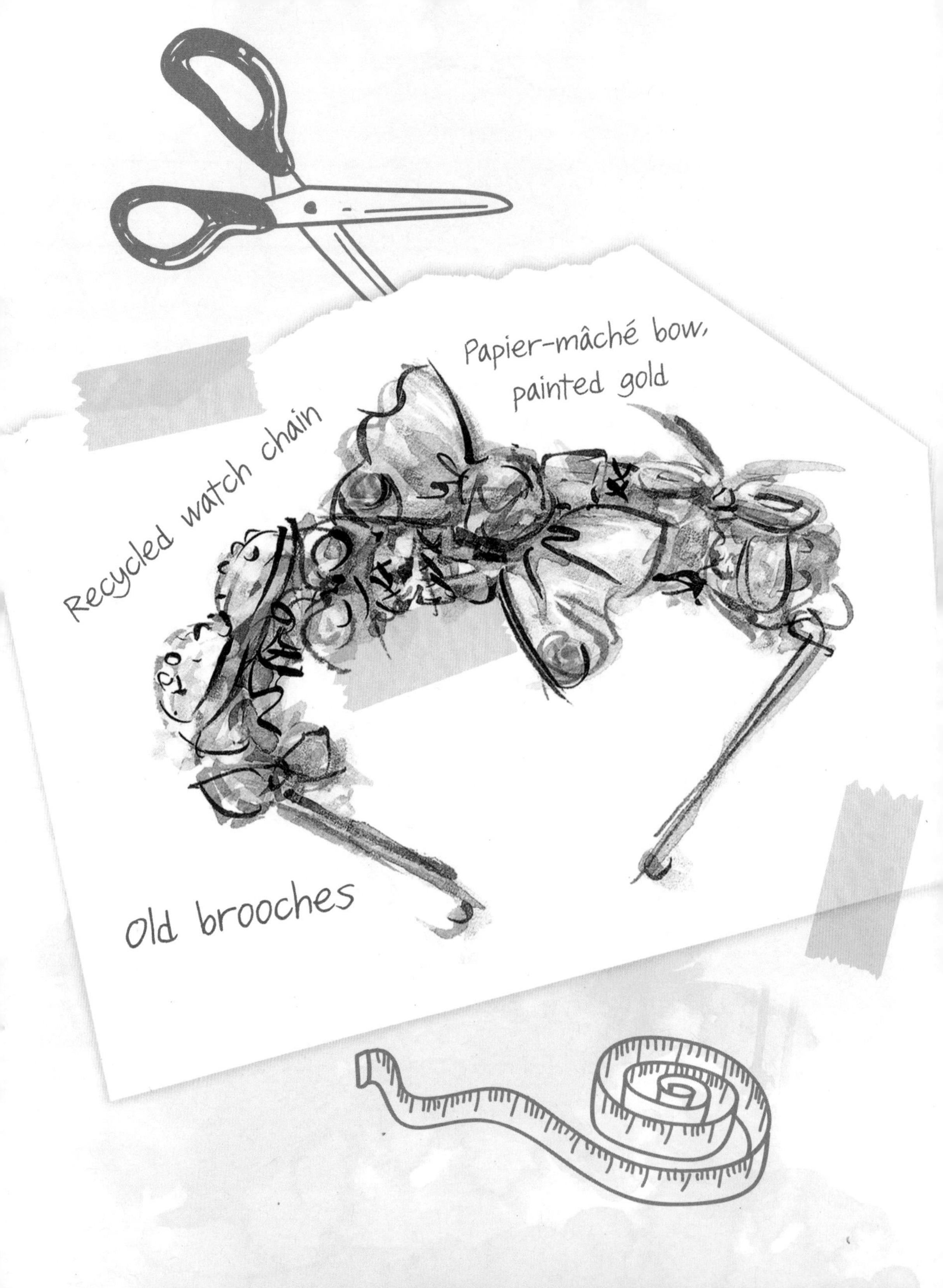
Papier-mâché bow,
painted gold
Recycled watch chain
Old brooches

Heart rhinestones
Simple gold
crown comb

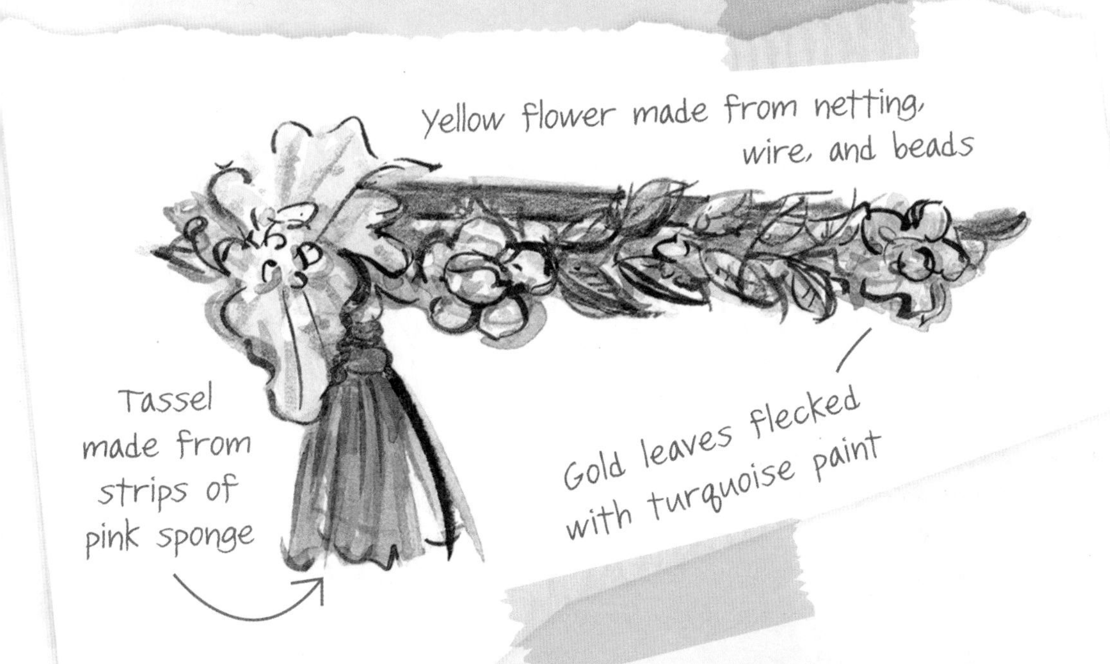
Yellow flower made from netting,
wire, and beads
Tassel
made from
strips of
pink sponge
Gold leaves flecked
with turquoise paint

COTILLION COVERAGE

I never actually thought anything would happen with my headpieces. I started making them when things were slow at the salon and I'd already swept and mopped the floors, scrubbed the sinks, wiped down the mirrors, washed and dried all the towels, folded the capes, and counted the cash in the register (Granny's list of chores is a mile long). Sometimes I gave them to different customers as gifts, and I had two that I always wore with special outfits.

Obviously I was really excited that Evie took some back to Auradon Prep with her, but I just thought she'd wear them sometimes, or maybe she'd give them to a few friends. So when I sat down to watch the Cotillion coverage on the Auradon News Network, I was just chomping away at some stale popcorn, not expecting much. I was so excited to see all the different genius designs Evie had come up with, sure, but I never in a million centuries expected her to wear the headpiece I had made. Or tell the reporters who I was. I yelped so loudly Granny told me to keep it down. So I just freaked out to myself, quietly.

It was like my life had officially started!

People in Auradon were talking about ME!!

AURADON WEEKLY

Mysterious "DIZZY OF THE ISLE" Finally Identified

After Cotillion last week, all of Auradon was asking the same question: Who is Dizzy of the Isle? The avant-garde designer is responsible for the one-of-a-kind headpieces worn by Lady Mal, Evie, Jane, Lonnie, and other Cotillion attendees.

Sources have revealed the mysterious designer as young Dizzy Tremaine, daughter of Drizella Tremaine and granddaughter of Lady Tremaine. The original pieces were created in her grandmother's

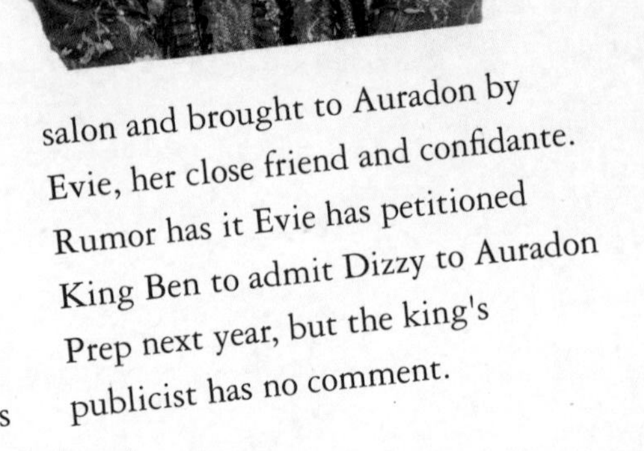

salon and brought to Auradon by Evie, her close friend and confidante. Rumor has it Evie has petitioned King Ben to admit Dizzy to Auradon Prep next year, but the king's publicist has no comment.

Who is "DIZZY OF THE ISLE"?

The Story Behind Auradon's New Accessories Designer

At last night's Cotillion, the world was introduced to fashion hair accessories. These one-of-a-kind items are made with found objects like keys, watch parts, and rusted gears. They come in the form of clips, combs, and headbands. Each accessory is a small but intricate piece of art, like the one worn by Evie, Auradon Prep's resident fashionista, in the photo below.

When asked about her latest creations, Evie was quick to give credit to a mysterious new designer. "These are by Dizzy of the Isle!" she announced to the crowd. But Evie disappeared onto the yacht before we could get more information. At the time of publication, we still hadn't heard back from her for further comment.

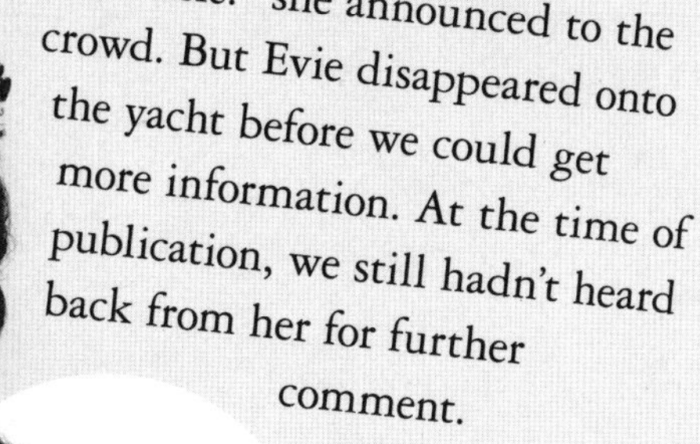

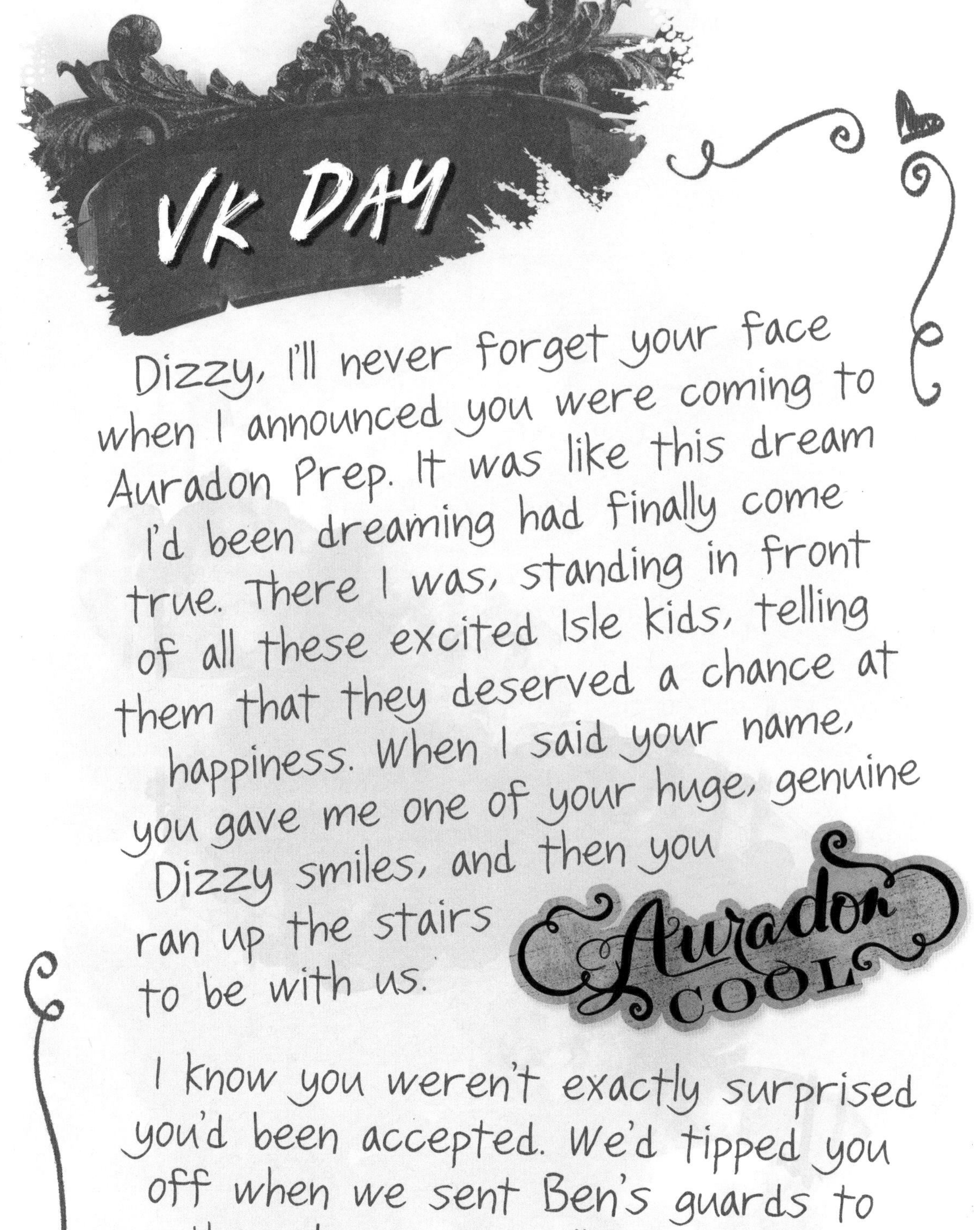

VK DAY

Dizzy, I'll never forget your face when I announced you were coming to Auradon Prep. It was like this dream I'd been dreaming had finally come true. There I was, standing in front of all these excited Isle kids, telling them that they deserved a chance at happiness. When I said your name, you gave me one of your huge, genuine Dizzy smiles, and then you ran up the stairs to be with us.

I know you weren't exactly surprised you'd been accepted. We'd tipped you off when we sent Ben's guards to the salon to formally invite you.

But still, I was so glad you got to have your moment to shine. Everyone knew why you were the first to be let in—you've always been so hardworking, so sweet, and so good. When I left for Auradon, you were happy for me, and you always celebrated my wins like they were your own. No one I know is kinder, gentler, or better.

HOME IS WHERE THE HEART IS

Auradon Prep is so beautiful. You know what the best part of my new life in Auradon is? Getting my own room in Evie's starter castle. The castle is amaaaaaaaazing, with spiral staircases and a turret and trees in every direction. It's like living in one of those big fairy-tale forests I've read about in books.

Some days Evie and I plop down in front of the TV and watch a marathon of The Princesses of East Riding. Other days we bake chocolate chip cookies or spend the afternoon in Evie's studio. I work on my headpieces, and she's at her sewing machine whipping up design masterpieces.

Hours will go by and then I'll look up and it'll be nighttime. We'll have to turn the lights on because we've been so excited about our projects we've been working in the dark.

I feel just as at home here as I did on the Isle. My granny's place was really nice by Isle standards, but I always had to work when I was there. Everything was about counting and recounting the cash in the register or wiping down the stations so they looked perfect for the next day's customers.

I think I really love it here.

Castle Rules
1. Be as messy as you want.
2. Stay up as late as you want.
3. Eat whatever you want.
4. Pursue your passion.
5. Make new friends.
6. Stay true to yourself.
7. Be happy.